About the Author

Heather Thurmeier was born and raised in the Canadian prairies, but now she lives in upstate New York with her own personal romance hero (aka her husband) and their two little princesses. When she's not busy taking care of the kids and an adventurous puppy named Indy, Heather's hard at work on her next romance novel. She loves to hear from readers. *Heart, humor, and a happily ever after…*

Website:
http://heatherthurmeier.com

Facebook:
Heather-Thurmeier-author/198113000212695

Twitter:
@hthurmeier

Blog:
http://heatherthurmeier.com/

Email:
heatherthurmeier@gmail.com

> For my mum,
> Thanks to you, I've always had a perfect example of just how strong a woman can be. My heroines are the way they are because of you.
> Heather Thur—

Love on Landing

HEATHER THURMEIER

A MEADOW RIDGE Romance

SILVER PUBLISHING
Published by Silver Publishing
Publisher of Erotic Romance

For my mum,

Thanks to you, I've always had a perfect example of just how strong a woman can be. I feel lucky as hell every day because of you.

Kathleen

If you purchased this book without a cover you should be aware that this book is stolen property. It was reported as "unsold and destroyed" to the publisher, and neither the author nor the publisher has received any payment for this "stripped book."

SILVERPUBLISHING

ISBN 978-1-61495-475-0

Love on Landing

Copyright © 2012 by Heather Thurmeier
Editor: Venus Cahill
Cover Artist: Reese Dante

All rights reserved. Except for use in any review, the reproduction or utilization of this work in whole or in part in any form by any electronic, mechanical or other means, now known or hereafter invented, including xerography, photocopying and recording, or in any information storage or retrieval system, is forbidden without the written permission of the editorial office, Silver Publishing, 18530 Mack Avenue, Box 253, Grosse Pointe Farms, MI 48236, USA.

All characters in this book have no existence outside the imagination of the author and have no relation whatsoever to anyone bearing the same name or names. They are not even distantly inspired by any individual known or unknown to the author, and all incidents are pure invention.

Visit Silver Publishing at https://spsilverpublishing.com

Note from the Publisher

Dear Reader,

Thank you for your purchase of this title. The authors and staff of Silver Publishing hope you enjoy this read and that we will have a long and happy association together.

Please remember that the only money authors make from writing comes from the sales of their books. If you like their work, spread the word and tell others about the books, but please refrain from copying this book in any form. Authors depend on sales and sales only to support their families.

If you see "free shares" offered or cut-rate sales of this title on ebook pirate sites, you can report the offending entry to copyright@spsilverpublishing.com

Thank you for not pirating our titles.

Lodewyk Deysel
Publisher
Silver Publishing
http://www.spsilverpublishing.com

Dedication

Dear friends, family and readers,

This story is about following your dreams. Thank you for your continued support so that I can follow my dream and share stories like this one with you.

Trademarks Acknowledgement

The author acknowledges the trademarked status and trademark owners of the following wordmarks mentioned in this work of fiction:

Vespa: Piaggio & C. S.p.A. Corporation Italy
Louis Vuitton: Louis Vuitton Malletier Corporation France
Dior: Christian Dior Couture
Chanel: Chanel, Inc.
Facebook: TheFacebook, Inc.
Prada: Prefel S.A. Corporation

Chapter One

Tali Radcliff leaned her head back against the headrest and gazed out the window. Raindrops splattered onto the double-paned glass blurring her view of the runway. Not that she could look past her sad, pathetic reflection anyway.

The reflection staring back at her turned the raindrops to tears on her cheeks and she instinctively wiped them away, only to find her cheeks sensitive and slightly swollen. She sighed and closed her eyes, desperately trying to block out the urge to start crying again. Instead, she focused on the white noise of the engines revving as the jet picked up speed for takeoff.

Her body was pushed harder into the back of the soft, cream-colored leather seat, her stomach falling as the wheels of the aircraft left the solid tarmac below. The jet crept higher and higher, increasing the distance between Tali and the life she would temporarily leave behind—the heartache she tried so hard to forget.

If only it were as easy as a little distance.

"Don't do it," she whispered. "You left your tears in your bedroom, where they belong." *A beauty queen never cries unless she's got a shiny new tiara on her head and a bouquet of fragrant flowers in her arms.*

It was a good rule of thumb to remember, one she'd learned long ago and tried to stick to at all cost. Of course, sometimes she had to give in and cry, but not often. Tali wasn't a crier, she was far too feisty to give in to silly tears.

But sometimes tears came no matter how hard she fought against them. Like when her boyfriend Roger broke up with her for no good reason and was then spotted with Samantha two hours later. Yep. That was a good reason to cry.

Roger can suck it.

Tali opened her eyes when the aircraft

leveled out as it reached its cruising altitude and grabbed her bag, dragging it onto the seat next to her. The shiny silver clasps clinked together on the seat as she pulled out her laptop. She flipped it open and signed on to her private in-flight Wi-Fi service.

She clicked on the Facebook icon on her home screen and scrolled through her news feed. Halfway down the page, her gaze froze and her heartbeat thundered in her ears. No frickin' way.

Roger Wilcox is engaged to Samantha Swanson.

"I'm going to kill her. I'm going to kill him." She slammed the laptop closed again and tossed it back into the bag.

How could he? How could he already be engaged to Samantha—Samantha Swanson of all people!—when he'd only broken up with Tali a couple of days ago? How does anyone fall in love so fast?

Little two-timing jackoff. He had to have been cheating on me. That's how.

That had to be it. There could be no other reason for two people to get engaged when one of them had "loved" someone else a mere forty-eight hours earlier.

She'd only known one couple to fall in love that fast—Chase and Julia. They'd met at a club one night then Julia had become his new employee by accident a few days later. They'd fallen in love practically overnight. Tali had been so happy for them, and she'd hoped to find love herself. Then Roger came along and she thought he was the one.

Tali didn't believe in fairytale love anymore. Love didn't happen in only a few days. She wasn't even sure she believed in a love of any kind after all this crap she'd recently been through with Roger.

She fixed her tailored cotton blouse, pulling the edges of the material taut and smoothing out the invisible wrinkles. Well good for them. They were perfect for each other. Roger was a cocky asshole and Samantha would make a perfect accessory at the Yacht club.

Tali never did like sailing anyway. All those waves usually made her feel queasy and when she mixed the waves with champagne cocktails, each day at sea became a disaster waiting to happen. Leaning over the railing of a ship, puking wasn't her most favorite position to be in with a man. Nope. Puke was no one's friend.

So this was good. She was good. They were good. Everything's great.

Tali's chin threatened to quiver, but she clenched her jaw. She would not cry over Roger again. Period. End of story. Moving on.

Speaking of moving, they'd only been in the air for a little while but her body already ached like it had been immobile for hours. She needed to clear her head, and since she couldn't, she would stretch her legs instead. She inhaled deeply, steadying her nerves and squashing her feelings back down where they belonged.

There weren't many options of where to walk on the small private jet. She wandered to the back galley to talk to Sara the flight attendant, but she wasn't there. The little window above the handle on the lavatory door was red.

Probably reading a book in there.

She could've kicked herself for forgetting her novel. She'd been in such a hurry to pack her things and get to her flight she'd left her half-read book on her bedside table. She still had a couple of magazines tucked into her bag from her last trip to the beach, but she tired quickly of the glossy photos on every page illustrating a very small amount of text. Trashy tabloid magazines never held her attention for long.

Tali groaned and wandered back through

the plane to the front of the aircraft. If Sara didn't want to talk to her, at least Edgar would.

Edgar had been her family's personal pilot for years and he always welcomed her into the cockpit for a visit during these long, boring, transatlantic flights. She had no idea how old he was, at least her father's age, but he was kind and always listened to her stories. Exactly what she needed right now—someone to listen to her, to tell her Roger was an idiot and she would be fine.

Tali rapped on the closed cockpit door before pulling it open and stepping inside. "How's it going in here, Edgar?" She grabbed his arm, squeezing gently.

He must be working out more. His biceps seemed larger and firmer than she expected them to. *Lucky Mrs Edgar.*

"I'm not Edgar." The pilot turned, eying her up and down. "What are you doing in my cockpit?"

Tali's mouth dropped open as she quickly took her hand back and crossed her arms in front of her chest. The man staring at her with intense brown eyes was not Edgar.

Oh no. Edgar was old. This man was not old. He was her age. And hot. No, make that gorgeous.

She cleared her throat. "I should be the one asking you the questions." She turned to the co-pilot Cameron and was relieved to see his familiar face smiling back at her.

"Hey, Tali," Cameron said.

"Hey, Cam," she replied. "Who is this guy? What happened to Edgar?"

"Didn't your father tell you? Edgar retired. This is Captain Taylor. He'll be flying with us from now on."

Tali turned her attention back to the pilot. Her cheeks grew hot as she processed this information about Edgar and the new—ahem, sexy—pilot. Why wouldn't her father tell her to expect a new pilot so she wouldn't make a fool of herself? Didn't he realize how much she hated change when it was sprung on her like this? How much she hated being left out of the loop so she'd inevitably end up feeling stupid?

"I wasn't told there would be someone new flying my plane."

The man laughed and shook his head. "Your plane, huh? You Meadow girls are all the same," he mumbled under his breath.

Her mind instantly thought of Samantha and her recent indiscretions. Tali could be a lot of things, but a cheater wasn't one of them.

He did not just lump me together with girls like Samantha.

"The last time I checked," the pilot continued, "I was the one sitting in the driver's seat, so I'm pretty sure that makes it my plane, at least for the duration of the flight. Now I'm going to have to ask you to leave since it's against FAA laws to have passengers in the cockpit while the aircraft is in flight."

Oh no. There was no way she was going to give up control of her own plane that easily. He might be the hired pilot, but it was still her damn plane. The initial sting of impending tears prickled her eyes. She clenched her jaw and steadied herself with a deep breath through her nose.

She made her voice as calm as possible. "My family's monogram is on the tail of this plane. I'm pretty sure that makes it mine along with anything in it, including you."

He stared at her without speaking before closing his eyes and rubbing his fingers in circles, massaging his temples. "So you want to have a pissing contest with me at thirty thousand feet? Great. Let me pull over for a minute so I can stroke your ego."

Tali sucked in a breath. This had nothing to do with her ego. If it had anything to do with that, he'd be talking about her shoes since she felt completely trampled after the last twenty-four hours and her shoes were the only ego-worthy thing left about her. "Where do you get off being a jerk to the girl who signs your checks?"

This man was infuriating, whoever the hell he was. Where did he get off speaking to her like this? No one spoke to her this way. Not if they wanted to keep their jobs.

He smiled and a small dimple appeared in his cheek. The sight of it made her feel like swooning. She'd never swooned for anyone, for any reason before. Damn it. She wasn't about to start swooning now. She placed her hand on the back of the co-pilot's chair to steady her equilibrium and her will.

Tali glared her challenge at the pilot, trying desperately not to notice the flecks of dark stubble along his strong jaw. How the man had stubble when it was barely mid-afternoon, she had no idea, but damn it looked good on him.

So. Damn. Good.

"I'm pretty sure it's your daddy's signature on the bottom of my checks so why don't you go back to your seat, read a trashy celebrity magazine and rest your pretty little head until we land in Paris. Leave the work to me, sweetheart."

Tali huffed. How dare he insinuate she had nothing better to do than sit and read the trashy celebrity magazine tucked away in her handbag?

He might be right, but he was still a jerk. She looked him over, sizing him up before answering and noticed his nametag read Gavin.

Gavin. Sounds like an asshole-y kind of name.

"How do you know this isn't a business trip to Paris, *Gavin*? How do you know I'm not sitting back there working on important documents instead of assuming I'm reading a trashy magazine?"

A shiver of excitement tickled along her spine. Fighting with him was so infuriating and—exhilarating. Her pulse pounded in her ears, her hands almost shaking with the thrill of anticipation as she waited for his response.

"That's Captain Taylor to you." He smirked. "Are you reading documents? Are you going to Paris for business?"

Tali swallowed hard, but didn't break her eye contact with *Captain Taylor*. Never let them smell your fear, right? Or was that only for wild animals and not incredibly sexy looking pilots?

"Well no," she said quietly. "I'm not actually looking at documents, but I am going to Paris for business."

Sure, business.

Getting over a jerk like Roger was really hard work and she absolutely needed a private meeting with Dior and Chanel. This business was critical to her mental wellbeing.

Totally counts.

Besides, nothing made her feel better than when she shopped for outfits for her little cousins. And there just so happened to be a super cute baby boutique down the street from Chanel. After she picked out a few outfits for them, there was no harm in stopping into Chanel for a few new outfits for herself. In fact it would be rude to Chanel not to stop by.

See, public relations—totally business.

A crooked eyebrow raise from Gavin told her he didn't believe her story about business meetings. She cleared her throat as she held his calculating gaze steady. She didn't have to prove anything to him. She did nothing but sit in boring business meeting usually. This was her trip, her *vacation* and she wasn't going to feel guilty about it.

Damn those eyes of his were incredible. The longer she gazed at them, the more she couldn't look away. It was as if his eyes were polar opposites of hers—drawing her gaze into his with an invisible, unbreakable force field. Her breathing hitched under the unfamiliar intensity.

"I'm sure your business with your personal shopper will be very ground breaking. Now if you'll excuse me, I really should focus on actually getting us to Paris." He turned his back to her and adjusted a few dials on the dashboard in front of him.

The guy was something else. Did he have a strong desire to stand in the unemployment line when they got back to the US? Because at the rate he was going, she had every intention of reporting him to her father. She may not sign the checks, but she had her father wrapped nicely around her little finger.

She spun on her heels and slammed the cockpit door on her way out. Sara glanced up from where she was now sitting in the seat across the aisle from Tali's seat.

"Everything okay?" Sara asked, placing her novel in her lap. "You sounded mad at the door."

"Peachy. Thanks. Can I get a diet soda, please?"

Sara put her novel aside and walked to the galley in the back of the jet, leaving Tali alone with her thoughts. Angry, annoyed thoughts.

She sat with a huff and pulled out the celebrity magazine she'd brought with her. She didn't give a damn if he saw her reading the magazine at this point. This was her plane. He was working for her family. She could do what she wanted without worrying about what he thought of her reading habits or vacation choice. If she wanted to shop until she dropped, that was her business.

Flipping a few pages, she tried to get interested in what the hottest celebrities were wearing and what they most certainly shouldn't be wearing. That always cheered her up. Today however, all she saw when she stared at the pictures were images of Gavin smirking at her with an expression of "I knew it" on his face.

"I don't like you," she whispered to the magazine, pretending the glossy photos were pictures of Gavin, then crammed it unceremoniously back into her bag.

Tali pulled out her sketchbook and a charcoal pencil, and flipped to the first clean page she found. As she began to draw, playing with the thickness of the line as she pushed harder or softer on the pencil, a wave of warmth washed over her. Her heartbeat faded back into her subconscious, her hands stopped shaking, and her breathing came in slow steady breaths.

Finally, for the first time in days, she felt marginally in control again.

Gavin groaned as the cockpit door slammed. "Wow. Seriously, what the hell is with that girl?"

Another stuck-up girl from the Meadow to make my life complicated.

"You better watch your mouth around Tali. She doesn't react well when people push her buttons. She can be a real firecracker."

"Come on, Cameron. You can't possibly be afraid of that princess. She's a marshmallow."

Cameron laughed. "Be afraid, dude. Be very afraid. If you think she's just a princess, you are so wrong."

Gavin knew she was more than just a princess. She may initially come off as a beautiful and charismatic ball of fluff, but she was a ball-breaker in every other way. He could see the fire in her eyes as she met his gaze and challenged him. This girl wouldn't take shit from anyone, and certainly not from him. Knowing that fact almost made him want to push her buttons more. There was something strangely arousing about fighting with her.

Every time she fired back at him with hot words, he felt the stirring of something more.

Squelch it, dumbass. Hot words don't equal hot sex. No, more likely hot words would equal big headaches as always. He wouldn't let another Meadow girl take advantage of him. When the whole "pilot" novelty wore off, he'd be left empty handed and out of a job again. This time, he was keeping his distance and his job. He wouldn't be anyone's toy—or slave.

He'd been warned to watch out for the boss's daughter, but somehow he'd imagined her being a bit different. He had expected Tali to be like the other rich girls he was used to. The girls who simply got their nails done and went shopping and otherwise remained fairly quiet—seen and not heard, that type. He hadn't expected a girl who would stand up for herself. A girl with fire and fight.

He liked this unexpected twist. A lot.

This girl with the feisty personality was

someone he could imagine spending time with. Except for one small problem—she annoyed the crap out of him. How was it, someone who looked so sweet and innocent could spar with him so effortlessly? And why did he enjoy interacting with her so much when all he really wanted to do was ignore her?

A smile played on Gavin's lips again at the thought of Tali's hip pushed to one side as she stood before him, challenging him. Good thing he knew better than to get involved with a princess. Some unsuspecting poor bastard was going to be in for a ride getting involved with her.

No thanks. He shook his head. Better to stay away from that mistake.

He was free and he wanted to stay that way. No way would he ever allow himself the chance to get mixed up with a girl like Tali—no matter how smokin' hot she was.

"Listen," Cameron started, "if I were

you, I'd keep my opinions to myself from now on when it comes to Tali. That girl can make your life in this job a living hell if you let her. I don't know about you, but I think this job is too cushy to risk messing it up by pissing off Tali."

"She can attempt to make my life as awful as she wants. But if she thinks I'm going to kiss her ass because she's the boss's daughter, well she's in for a harsh reality. Besides, if the Radcliffs don't want me to fly for them because I won't suck up to the girl, well then there's always another rich family who will want me."

I can't wait to have my own charter company. Then I'll choose who I fly.

"Whatever you say, dude. It's your life."

"Exactly. Which is why I'm not going to let some spoiled brat make me her slave."

Gavin flipped a switch and leaned back into his chair to relax as the plane flew itself on autopilot for a while. He closed his eyes and sighed, enjoying the silence filling the small space. A few more hours and they'd land in Paris. Then he'd be free of Tali while she shopped her heart out.

He planned to enjoy every single second of Tali-free time he got until she snapped her fingers for him to bring her back stateside.

Chapter Two

Gavin stood on the top step of the stairway leading down to the tarmac below and took a deep breath of air, filling his lungs as he stretched his arms above his head. Nothing compared to those first few breaths of fresh air after a long flight. He loved to fly, but he hated the recirculated air onboard. He slowly exhaled with a sigh.

"You gonna stand there all night stargazing or do you plan on moving sometime soon?" Tali's voice behind him was as crisp as the early-evening air.

Without a word, he stepped aside.

"Thank you." She brushed passed him, her flowery perfume scenting her wake. "Would you grab my bag, please?"

Well, at least she asked nicely.

He stepped back into the cabin of the plane and opened the storage closet nearest the cockpit. Tucked inside sat her Louis Vuitton luggage. Only one piece.

She packs light.

Gavin hauled her suitcase out of the cabin and down the narrow metal stairs. For a small suitcase, the bag was surprisingly heavy. At the bottom of the stairs sat two more pieces of luggage, which must have been retrieved by the ground crew from the underbelly of the plane. A memory of counting bags clicked in his brain. Of course they'd been hers. No way did a girl like Tali travel light.

Figures.

"This way," she said. She spun on her heel and walked off with only her handbag slung on her shoulder.

Gritting his teeth, he propped her smaller bag on top of one of the larger ones and his overnight bag onto the other and followed her. He only had to put up with her for a few more minutes and then he'd be free to lounge, undisturbed in his own room. She could be across town in her fancy five-star hotel ordering around the bellhop and he would happily grab a greasy burger at the two-star airport hotel bar. Perfect. If she took a week to finish her "business" before she called him to fly her home, that would be fine with him—as long as he wasn't expected to spend the week at her beck and call.

Tali stopped in the customs line with her passport in hand, grumbling under her breath and looking from one customs agent to another. Gavin simply stood still waiting and shuffled forward as the line inched ahead.

"So, any idea how many days you'll need until you'll be ready to head stateside again?"

Tali shrugged. "Not sure. Why, you ready to go back? We just got here."

She had her head turned to look at him and didn't seem to notice the line had moved again while they spoke. As he placed his hand on the small of her back to suggest she step forward with the line, a flash of electricity shot through him.

Instantly Tali's eyes flickered up to meet his and he pulled his hand back, shoving it into his pocket where he would be safe from any more unwanted shocks. He hadn't felt something like this before—this current of energy passing between them. The feeling wasn't bad exactly. In fact it was a great feeling, one that made him feel stirrings of something more below his waist.

But he didn't want to feel this—whatever this emotion was—for Tali.

She was a spoiled brat. And he wanted nothing more to do with her than fly her around the globe at her whim. She could walk her Pradas all over whomever the hell she wanted to, but that someone wouldn't be him. Nope.

"I'm in no rush to go back." He cleared his throat, getting his thoughts back in order and off of her. "I was only curious how long I'd be hanging around the airport."

She glanced down at her hands before meeting his gaze. "Why don't you come stay at the hotel with me. Well, not with me—but you know, at the same hotel—but in your own room." Her gaze flickered away from his and focused instead on her hands as she wrung them together tightly, almost as if she were suddenly nervous.

He smiled as her cheeks turned a subtle hue of pink with her words. *A crack in the hard shell?* "Thanks, but I'll be fine at the hotel here."

A loose strand of hair fell across Tali's face as she stepped forward with the line. Without thinking, he tucked it behind her ear, his thumb brushing against her cheek accidentally. Another shot of electricity coursed through him and he smiled in response before quickly pulling his hand back.

Damn it. Stop that.

"I'll charge your room to mine so the cost won't inconvenience you," she offered quietly.

That's generous. But he couldn't accept. "You don't have to worry about me."

"Actually, I was sort of worrying about myself."

"Shocker." He muttered under his breath, but when he saw her hand tighten around her passport he realized she'd heard him. Oops.

"I only meant I normally don't travel alone, especially not to foreign countries. I thought having you nearby might be nice so I wouldn't feel so alone."

Tali turned to face the front of the line, which had disappeared as they'd chatted. She shifted her weight back and forth as she stood on the white line waiting in silence.

He should say something. He hadn't thought travelling alone would bother her. If being alone was a problem for her, why hadn't she brought a girlfriend on the trip? Hell, why hadn't she brought her boyfriend with her if she was really so worried about staying in a strange country, in a strange hotel room by herself?

"Next," a customs agent called from a few booths away.

Gavin watched as Tali wandered off to the booth and handed her passport across the counter. She looked so confident and sure of herself, standing there smiling and batting her eyes as she answered the man's questions. He never would have guessed she was uncomfortable. Or lonely.

Gavin stepped up to the nearest booth when he was called forward. He showed his passport and his airline credentials, answered a few quick questions, and before he even had a chance to get uncomfortable, the agent stamped his passport. He took his identification back and crossed into the luggage area to wait for Tali.

As he watched, Tali started shifting her

weight back and forth again from one foot to the other. She turned her head toward the line-up and then quickly scanned the booths before settling on him in the baggage claim area. He was almost certain he saw her shoulders drop and a sigh escape her mouth as her gaze rested on him. Her head snapped back to the customs agent as he spoke and she grinned as she retrieved her passport and quickly walked away from the counter.

Why was she so seemingly uncomfortable on a trip she wanted to take? Maybe she really did need someone with her, well nearby at least.

She crossed over to Gavin with her carry-on luggage in tow behind her. "Do you mind helping me get my bags to a car before you leave me?"

Leave her? He wasn't exactly abandoning her. "Sure."

He grabbed her bags and together they

left the customs area. Right outside the security doors, a man stood with a large whiteboard with Tali's name scrawled across the surface in thick black marker.

"I guess he can help me with my bags from here." Tali motioned toward the driver with a curt nod. "I don't want to keep you from whatever plans you had here at the airport."

Damn it. She looked so defeated. Did she always have those big bags under her eyes or were they something new? Rich girls usually looked completely put together at all times, but now when he got a better look at her, she wasn't done up at all. In fact, she looked like crap. What was wrong with her? Had she been crying on the flight? Why?

Damn it again.

"It's okay. I'll go," he said.

"No really. You don't have to. I forgot there would be a driver to help me with my bags, so you're officially off-duty until otherwise notified."

"That's not what I meant." He sighed. Why was he agreeing to more frustration than he was paid to put up with? "I'll go to the hotel with you if you still want me to."

He thought her face might explode with the size of the smile that sprang to her lips. "Really?" She clapped. "That's awesome. Really awesome. I'm so excited!"

Gavin couldn't help but smile while watching her bounce around excitedly. Her enthusiasm was contagious. "Okay, okay. That's enough. Let's not get too carried away. I said I'd stay at the hotel with you. It's not like I agreed to fill in for your girlfriends and go shopping with you or anything."

Her eyes widened. "Oh, shopping. That's a great idea. Let's do that tomorrow after the jetlag wears off."

He shook his head. "No. No way." He waved his hand at her to make his point. "I agreed to the hotel change. I did not agree to shopping. No."

"Oh come on. It's fun to walk around Paris and window shop."

"I think that sounds like torture, not fun."

"What else are you going to do at the hotel while you wait for me? Watch French television? 'Cause that sounds like a whole lot of fun."

"Maybe I will. Or maybe I'll stay in bed. Or maybe I'll go out to eat. Or maybe I'll go to the Louvre. I don't know yet. I do know I will *not* be going shopping while in Paris."

Tali's dark eyes twinkled like the night sky. "Well, we'll see what tomorrow brings now won't we." She turned on her heel and followed the driver out to the black town car waiting in a parking stall near the front doors.

Great. He had to open his big mouth and give her the idea of him coming with her while she walked around Paris, spending money and buying new things she surely didn't need. Way to go, big guy.

    Tali handed over her black credit card to the front desk clerk at the hotel. She tapped her nails on the counter as she waited for the man to swipe her card and give her the room keys for herself and Gavin. Her heart did a quick somersault in her chest at the thought of him staying near her.

    She was glad he'd changed his mind and decided to stay with her. She wasn't used to travelling completely alone and since she'd left the States so quickly, no one had been available to join her. Staying in the hotel room alone was fine, but being completely alone in the city was a little more than she could currently handle. Knowing Gavin was safely down the hall from her would put her at ease so she could rest and relax enough to put Roger behind her for good.

She was happy to know Gavin was here if she needed him.

Sure, Gavin had been a bit of an ass on the flight, but he was also a pretty fine piece of eye-candy. Even though his comments had been completely uncalled for—albeit correct—sparring with him in the plane had been strangely exhilarating. And seeing the dimple in his cheek still made her feel slightly lightheaded.

Strange.

She didn't usually have such visceral reactions to people. She was usually a more calculated romantic. She wasn't one of those girls who got swept off her feet by every man who glanced in her direction. Nope.

She turned away plenty of hot guys without a second thought, so what was it about this guy that made her want him near her even if it meant she was going to have to put up with more of his mouthy comments?

"Here are your keys, *Mademoiselle*." The man behind the counter handed her two sets of keycards. "You are in room 318 and *Monsieur* Taylor is in room 350. Please enjoy your stay with us at the hotel and don't hesitate to ring us if you need anything at all to make your stay more comfortable. *Bonsoir*."

"*Merci*." She took the keys and handed one to Gavin.

Gavin Taylor. Nice. Tali Taylor. Could be even nicer—stop.

There was no way "Tali Taylor" was ever going to happen. He was not her type of guy. She only had marriage on her mind because of seeing Roger's stupid engagement to Samantha plastered all over Facebook.

She didn't want to get married yet. Ever. Okay well, maybe that wasn't entirely true. Maybe she did want to get married one day but she wasn't going to get married to some asshole like Roger.

And she certainly wouldn't marry some jerky, smart-mouthed pilot like Gavin either.

"Here you go." Gavin set her bags in front of her room door. "I'm pretty sure you can handle it from here right?"

She nodded. "Sure. Of course."

She unlocked her door and pushed it open with her foot, grabbing her bags by the pull handles and tugged them together toward the door. The bags collided with the doorframe with a noisy thud.

"Oops." She giggled, backing up the bags and giving them another tug toward the door, which was now crushing her toes as they poked out the tip of her very strappy sandals.

Gavin sighed. Loudly.

"Oh just let me do it already." He strode forward and grabbed the two bags from her hands.

She stepped back against the door, holding it open with her body instead of her poor sore toes. Gavin pulled the luggage back out into the hallway and maneuvered one bag so it pointed forward in front of him, and dragged the other behind him. As he passed through the doorway, his shoulder glided past her with only an inch to spare. She inhaled a fleeting whiff of his cologne and a stirring of butterflies came to life in her stomach as she gripped the door handle tightly to steady her suddenly nervous knees.

Roger had never smelled that good.

She forced herself away from the door and into the room. She didn't want to stand there like an idiot, gawking at him. Instead, she crossed the room and sat down on the bed, slipping off her sandals and rubbing her feet.

"Thanks again for staying here with me and helping me with my bags and everything."

Gavin shrugged setting the bags on the luggage racks against the wall. "Sure. I don't know what you would have done without me."

He turned to face her with his arms crossed. "Anything else you want me to take care of for you before I give in to jetlag and hit the sack? Fix your air conditioner or fluff your pillows?" He grinned as if he thought he was being funny.

He might smell great, but damn it, he was a total jerk.

Enough already, sexy-pilot guy. Enough.

"Why are you in such a huff? What is it? The super nice hotel you get to stay in for free? You'd rather stay in the crappy airport hotel than here because you had to help me with my bags for two seconds? Thank you so much for your valiant sacrifice. I don't know what I would have done without you."

"I just flew eight hours across the ocean you know, so excuse me if I'm not up to the usual pleasantries. I'm tired and I want to rest, not follow your sorry ass around, answering to your every whim. At least at the airport hotel, I wouldn't have to play bellboy to every spoiled brat I meet."

Tali sprang from the bed. How dare he? Her ass was anything but sorry.

"I am not a spoiled brat you pompous jerk. Just because I like to stay in a nice hotel and read a trashy tabloid magazine once in a while and go shopping doesn't mean I'm spoiled. And for your information, my ass is fabulous, thank you very much. You'd be lucky to have to follow it around all day."

She stared up at him, furious he would make her sound like a rich bitch. His dark eyes stared back down at her and his cheek dimple was nowhere to be seen with his jaw clenched tight. Damn he was tall when she wasn't in heels. He towered deliciously over her.

"My mistake," he started, "that sounds perfectly unspoiled."

He leaned down toward her and she caught another hint of his cologne in the air. The scent infiltrated her senses arousing her despite her anger. "And I'm well aware," he continued, "of how fabulous your ass is. I may be the pilot, but I always know my cargo. Now if you'll excuse me, I need to get some sleep."

"You did not just call my ass fat. My ass is not cargo."

He smirked and his dimple appeared. She suddenly wanted to lick it. How odd.

"If the jeans fit, babe." His smirk turned into a full-fledged grin. "Besides, lots of guys like a girl with a little—cargo."

Tali tried to find words to retort as she stared up at him. She knew she should fight back, but being so close to him, smelling his scent again, her brain malfunctioned. All she could think about were the dark pools staring back at her and the stubble along his jaw that was now thicker than it had been on the plane.

Stubble that so perfectly outlined his strong jaw, she wondered what it would feel like scratching against the skin of her neck if he were to kiss her at the tender spot behind her ear she loved so much. Was the spiky stubble as scratchy as it looked, or softer?

She pulled her hand back quickly from where it had been creeping up toward his face like it had a mind of its own. She took a step back from him, bumping into the edge of the bed and falling into a sitting position.

Her mind cleared now that she wasn't in such close proximity to him and the hurt from his words echoed in her mind. After the last few days of stress and heartache, being called a brat was exactly the last thing she could handle. Defeat settled into her chest, weighing her down until she couldn't get up off the bed if her room were on fire.

She wasn't a spoiled brat, but a jerk like Gavin would never find out. Maybe Roger thought she was a spoiled brat, too. Well, they could both go to hell.

Gavin could think whatever he wanted

about her. She knew who she was and if he was too ignorant to see the real her, then she wasn't going to bother trying to change his mind. If he thought she was spoiled, she would act spoiled.

"Just leave. I don't want to keep you from your big plans." She fought back the tears prickling her eyes. She didn't really want to cry again but the last couple of days were too much. The last thing she needed right now was to fight with Gavin. "Think whatever you want to about me, I don't care anymore. Just go."

Gavin stared at her for a moment as his posture relaxed. He appeared as if he was going to say something, but then decided against it.

She bit her lip while she waited for him to leave. The tears were on their way and she didn't want to let him see them. No, she wouldn't let him see them. "Please, go." Her voice was shakier than she wanted it to be, but she had no more control over it.

"Listen," he said, taking a step toward

her. "I'm sorry. I shouldn't have called you a spoiled brat. I—I didn't mean to make you upset."

"You didn't. It's nothing. I'm not upset." But the tear trickling down her cheek gave her away before she could hide her emotions.

"Ah crap. Really. I'm sorry. Don't cry."

"Leave me alone, Gavin. This has nothing to do with you. I promise I won't bother you again until I'm ready to go home. So thank you. Your bellboy services are no longer needed by this spoiled brat. I'll call you in a few days."

Gavin's brow creased as he clearly debated about what to do. Finally he strode to the door and opened it. "I'll check on you in the morning."

He disappeared through the doorway leaving her in silence that was quickly filled with hiccupping gasps as the tears fell uncontrollably.

CHAPTER THREE

"Shit, shit, shit." Gavin cursed under his breath as he walked down the hall to the room Tali had set him up with. He hadn't meant to call her spoiled. Even if she was actually unbelievably beyond spoiled, it wasn't his place to call her a brat.

He wasn't sure what had come over him. He never spoke to women that way. Ever. But there was something about Tali that absolutely infuriated him. Maybe it was her expectation that everything would go the way she wanted it to all the time. Or maybe it was because he found her incredibly attractive when all he really wanted was to find her ugly.

She certainly wasn't ugly. Damn it. Her dark hair begged to be tangled around his fingers as her tresses fell across her shoulders in long waves. And don't even get him started on her—ahem, cargo. She hadn't been lying when she said her ass was fabulous. He wholeheartedly agreed and it had taken every ounce of strength he'd had not to reach around behind her and grab a handful of her flesh when she'd brought her ass into their fight.

He wouldn't think about her ass. No matter how nice her butt was and how much it practically begged him to grab it, he would resist. He'd been a toy for far too many women like Tali and he wasn't going to fall into that trap again. He had to remember who she really was and try his best not get caught up in how much her cheeks flushed when she fought with him. She looked really good when she was hot and bothered…

Nope. He wouldn't go there. He'd sit in his room and rent French pay-per-view movies on her dime until she told him she was ready to go. Then he'd fly her home and try not to get into another fight with her. The silent treatment would be much better than tears.

He hadn't meant to be so hard on her. He certainly hadn't meant to make her cry. Had she really started to cry because he called her a spoiled brat? That didn't seem right at all. Maybe there was more going on with her than he realized. Maybe there was a bigger reason for her solo trip.

Tomorrow morning he would check to see how she was doing and once he knew she was okay then his commitment to her would be done until she wanted to go home. That was fair. He wasn't paid to babysit her, but he also couldn't walk away from her until he knew she was okay.

* * * *

Gavin rapped on the door to Tali's room and leaned against the doorframe as he waited for her. He didn't even know if she'd still be in bed or if she'd already left her room since he had no idea what kind of schedule the girl liked to keep.

He'd woken that day at mid-morning, allowing himself the luxury of sleeping in. He didn't usually suffer from jetlag thanks to the many miles he'd logged, but he did enjoy sleeping late the first day in a new time zone whenever possible. There was something refreshing about waking up somewhere new without a schedule. Life didn't get much better than exploring somewhere different and interesting every few days. He couldn't imagine any other way of life.

A mumbled sounded from inside the room but he couldn't make out the words. "Tali," he called. "You okay in there?"

Another muffled response answered him through the thick door, yet he still couldn't make out the words. Was she hurt? Still upset? Maybe she really was still sleeping?

"Tali, I can't come in unless you open

the door. Can you just let me know you're okay so I can go get breakfast?"

He didn't want to be rude, but honestly, he didn't feel like talking to her very much today. He didn't want to get into another argument with her if she was feeling fragile for some reason. And he definitely didn't want to be her impromptu shoulder to cry on. No thanks.

The lock slipped in the door and an instant later Tali stood on the other side—wrapped in a towel. Her bare shoulders were a warm ivory that looked like they had been perfectly polished by someone with great attention to detail. Her hair hung wet across her collarbone and his eyes couldn't help but follow the tiny rivers of water running off her tresses as they disappeared into her cleavage.

His eyes focused on the mounds of her breasts held captive under the tightly wrapped towel. He suddenly prayed the towel would come loose and fall to the floor so he could see the rest of the treasures she kept just out of his view.

He'd never hated a towel more in his life.

"Hey, Gavin. What's up?" Tali opened the door wide and pulled him through before letting it close behind him. "It's drafty out in the hallway."

He saw the goose bumps rise on her flesh and had to stop himself from reaching out to rub them away. They were so tempting. She was so tempting.

Stop. She's the same spoiled girl she was last night. He nodded unconsciously. *She's also naked.*

"I was just checking you out." His gaze flashed back to her face and away from the view clouding his thoughts and tying his tongue. "I— I meant to say I was just checking *on* you to see if you were okay since you seemed a bit upset last night."

She smiled and put her hands on her

hips. Her towel opened at her side slightly, revealing a glimpse of her milky-white thigh. "I'm fine. It's amazing what a good night's sleep and a hot shower can do for a person."

And a body.

"Great. I'm glad to hear that. So I'll leave you alone then." He started toward the door but her hand on his arm stopped him.

"Could you stay?" Her dark eyes gazed up at him and he wanted to say yes to her request.

"Why?"

"I thought maybe we could hang out together today. You know, walk around the city a bit. Maybe shop a little. Take in the sights. What do you say?"

"I say I have better things to do than carry your shopping bags all over the city."

"Really? Like what? Stay in the hotel and pout?"

He shrugged. He wasn't going to let her

get the better of him again. He wasn't going to let her get him worked up into another bickering match. "Maybe. But whatever I do on my time off is my business, not yours. And I don't pout."

"You seem awfully pouty," she said, turning away from him to walk back across the room. She grabbed the outfit lying on the bed and disappeared into the bathroom. "You're going to get bored if you stay inside all day," she called through the closed door.

"I think I'll manage just fine, thanks," he called back.

He glanced around the room. Her bed was still unmade. A half-full bottle of diet soda and an empty jar of salted cashews lay on the bedside table. The girl obviously didn't feel the need to clean up after herself. And who actually took food from the mini bar? That stuff was always way overpriced. Of course Tali probably didn't even consider prices, ever—of anything—least of all cashews from the mini bar.

Sure, not spoiled at all.

"I think you're being silly to miss out on everything Paris has to offer because of me. I'm not that bad, you know."

The bathroom door opened and Tali strode out looking even more amazing than she had the day before. Her long hair was twisted up into some kind of ponytail, allowing him a clear view of her neck, which was beautifully enticing. She wore a simple T-shirt that hugged her curves and a pair of jeans that looked like they'd been created for her ass alone.

Hot. Damn.

Maybe it wouldn't be the worst thing in the world to follow around a derriere like hers all day. But did he want to be her personal shopping bag holder? Did he want to listen to her whine about something silly while spending mountains of money on things she didn't need?

Tali turned and bent to slip her feet into a pair of boots, pulling them up to her knees over the skinny-legged jeans. He caught the slightest glimpse of a pink lacy thong peeking out from under the edge of her jeans.

Yes. Yes he did want to listen to her whine all day. *Sign me up.*

"Fine." He sighed. "I'll go."

"See, I knew you didn't want to stay here all day by yourself. Don't worry. We're going to have so much fun." She slid the zipper of her boot up to her knee and stood. A huge smile played along her lips and Gavin couldn't help but smile too. Tali buzzed around the room collecting her things.

"I have one condition though."

Tali stopped, her hand on her hip. "What?" He could hear the suspicion in her voice.

"I'll go to whatever stores you want, without complaint—"

"Great. Let's go." Tali took his hand and pulled him in the direction of the door. But he was bigger than her and there was no way he was moving until she agreed to his terms. He may not like shopping, but there was one thing he loved in Paris.

"I'm not finished." He held his ground and she stopped tugging on him, the warmth of her hand in his momentarily distracting him from his task.

He didn't want to think about Tali in that way, but he couldn't stop himself from wrapping his hand around her tiny one, trapping her heat. Her hand felt so small and delicate in his, a stark contrast to the huge feisty personality she presented. Her warmth radiated through him as he stood there, struggling to remember what he wanted to say.

"So... what? What's your big condition?" The edge in her voice broke through his confusion.

"If I follow you around all day, like a good boy then I get to choose where we go for dinner. No complaints from you."

Tali stuck out her bottom lip and tilted her head so she peered at him through her lashes. "But I've been looking forward to eating at my favorite restaurant since the moment we landed. I promise you'll love the food as much as I do."

He knew exactly what she was trying to do and he wasn't going to fall into her trap. She may be able to bend other people to her will with a simple bat of her long eyelashes, but not him. He wasn't falling for her act. She got her way with everything else, he wanted his way with dinner.

Maybe he wanted his way with her too. *No. Not worth the frustration.*

"My choice for dinner or I'm not shopping with you. Deal?"

He grinned as she narrowed her eyes at him. It felt good to be the one to make her bend a little. Maybe now she wouldn't expect him to do anything and everything she asked. He was her companion for the day and her pilot for the flight, but that did not mean he'd be at her beck and call. Maybe now she'd know where he stood.

"Fine. I'll eat wherever you say. Can you at least tell me where we're going?"

"Now what kind of fun would that be?" He laughed at her expression of annoyance. She was fun to tease. "I promise you'll love the food… If you give the restaurant a fair chance."

"I'm not so sure I like the sound of this."

This time he was the one pulling her toward the door. "Good. Then we're about even."

* * * *

Tali slid her hand along the smooth silk on the hanger. The material was sinfully luxurious and begged her to buy it. How could she refuse?

She pulled the hanger from the rack and held the dress up to examine the colors. The material of a garment had to be nice, but it was always the colors that made Tali reach for her credit card. This piece had exquisite hues in the delicate fabric—swirls of rich blues and greens intermingling on top of a cream backdrop. The way the colors combined and worked together took her breath.

"That one's pretty," Gavin said from beside her.

Pretty? Oh no. This piece was so much more than simply pretty. There wasn't even a word in the English language appropriate enough to describe the beauty of the simple dress.

"You going to try on the dress at some point?"

She shook her head. "You don't 'try on' something like this. I don't choose the dress, the dress will have to choose me."

Gavin choked on a laugh. "Okay. So will the dress be trying you on then because you've been standing here staring at it for about five minutes already and my feet are getting sore? I'm ready to try out the chairs in the waiting area and rate them. Do you think these ones will beat the ones at Dior?"

Tingles of annoyance sparked to life in her veins at his words. How could he possibly care about chairs when there were so many beautiful clothes to experience? It wasn't right.

"Go sit," she said, nodding toward the back of the boutique where the dressing rooms were. "I'll follow you."

Gavin walked off toward the oversized leather chairs she could see inside the waiting area. She followed, eying his nicely rounded ass for about the hundredth time. Now his was an ass worth following.

Oh my. A streak of bright red caught her

eye, peaking out from amongst a rack of black. Carefully separating the garments, she pulled the red free. Her breath caught in her throat as she stared at the gorgeous blouse. She could only cross her fingers and pray this shirt would also choose her.

A shiver of excitement caused goose bumps to rise along the surface of her skin as she dashed into a dressing room. She tore off her shirt, eager to feel the crimson material wrapped around her body.

Slipping the blouse over her head, she gently tugged the material down and into place. It felt amazing. Better than amazing. She held her breath as she turned to face the mirror. Would it look as good as it felt?

Better.

She pulled open the dressing room door and cleared her throat to get Gavin's attention. He glanced up from his phone quickly then back down, almost as if he hadn't really looked.

Slowly, his head tilted up to really gaze at her, his eyes unblinking.

"You look beautiful." He smiled dreamily at her.

"Thank you. Don't you love the cut of this?" She ran her hands over the blouse, smoothing out the material as it hugged her body like a second skin. The design was creative and unique. A plunging neckline created a deep V between her breasts, as small hand-stitched beads shimmered in waves with the light.

"The detail," she whispered. "These little details—" She couldn't even finish her thought, too distracted with examining every single inch of the blouse.

She walked back into the dressing room, carefully removing the blouse and hanging it safely on the far wall of the little room. She didn't want to risk accidentally bumping into it and harming it some way. She knew she was being silly, but she couldn't help feeling instantly protective of it.

Slipping into the dress, she gasped as the smooth silk caressed her skin. The blues and greens swirled along the fabric as she moved, mesmerizing her. She stared at herself in the mirror, unable to see anything except the beauty of the dress. The colors dancing on the dress were like gazing at an oil painting hanging in the Louvre—simply breathtaking.

Tali pulled open the dressing room door and stepped out to show Gavin, still feeling dazed. His eyes met hers and traveled down the length of her body. She suddenly felt naked under his gaze and the longer he looked at her, the quicker her pulse pounded.

She liked when he looked at her like a desirable woman instead of the spoiled brat he'd called her. She liked the way his eyes took in her curves—her breasts and hips especially accentuated by the cut of the dress. She wondered what it would be like to feel his hands roaming her body instead of his eyes. The thought made her feel even more lightheaded.

Gavin's gaze reached hers again and she could see his approval. He liked the dress on her that much was obvious.

She broke their gaze and did a little twirl, spinning a full rotation before stopping to face the mirror. She glanced back over her shoulder at him and smiled when she saw his eyes focus on her rear. Again.

Gavin stared at Tali's behind as she stared at herself in the mirror. Her curves and contours looked beyond amazing, hugged by the silken material. What he wouldn't do to tear it from her body and pull her onto the chair on top of him.

No. Can't.

He reluctantly pulled his gaze from her behind and settled on her reflection in the full-length mirror instead. She was stunning in the dress, that was a given. But the way she looked at herself was what really captured his attention. She acted as if she were in a dreamy state, tracing the swirls of color with her fingers across her flat stomach. Watching her was hypnotizing.

What was she thinking? She definitely didn't seem like a normal spoiled brat at that moment. A spoiled brat would look at the garment for about five second and ignore the price while they ran to the register with their purchases. But that's not what Tali did at all.

She appeared to be admiring the garment. Taking in even the littlest detail and examining each stitch of thread fully. He wished he could read her mind to know what she was thinking as she stared at it. She looked so thoughtful, so intellectual—so absolutely gorgeous.

"So," he started, trying to break the spell

in the room, "are you going to take that one? Seems a shame to leave it here when you obviously love it."

"I do love it. It's so perfect and imperfect at the same time."

He crinkled his forehead and took in the dress again. Nothing about the dress looked wrong. What was she talking about, imperfect?

"If there's something wrong with the dress, maybe you should leave it. You don't want to pay that kind of price for something with flaws."

She shook her head slowly. "Not flaws. Just—oh never mind. I can't explain what I mean." She stepped back into the dressing room, still shaking her head at him.

"What? You said it was imperfect. It looks fine to me."

"You don't understand. You don't see what I see."

Gavin got up from the chair and stood

beside her door, leaning against the frame as he waited. "I guess I don't." He shrugged. He didn't know if she was annoyed, upset, angry or simply disappointed he couldn't see the dress the same way she did. And he didn't understand why it bothered him.

He crossed his arms and leaned his head against the doorframe. He was exhausted after their flight the day before and he wondered how much longer Tali would want to shop before returning to the hotel. He hoped for a nap before dinner.

Gavin closed he eyes and yawned, letting out a long, slow breath.

"Nice," said Tali. "Just what I wanted to see, a close up of your tonsils."

He snapped his mouth shut and his eyes sprang open. Tali had opened her door and he hadn't heard her. Now she stood only a few short inches from him.

"Sorry," he started to say, but was

distracted by her eyes. They were even darker up close and under the florescent lights of the store—pools of liquid chocolate. Now that she hadn't cried for a few hours, the whites were crisp against the dark brown. There was a warmth growing inside of him as he realized how happy and relieved he was to see her eyes white instead of pink and puffy.

"What, no witty comment to make back at me this time? Just sorry? Lame." The corners of her lips pulled up into a sly smile, instantly reminding him of how feisty she really was. Beautiful, but feisty—a lethal combination to any man.

His mouth curved up to mirror hers. She did have an awfully nice mouth. He imagined what it would be like to touch it, to taste it, to feel her breath against his tongue. Gavin swallowed, finding his voice. "I guess I've gone brain dead from too much shopping to be able to make witty remarks anymore."

"Brain dead, huh?" She smirked at him and arched her eyebrow. "That didn't take much. Shopping isn't supposed to be a contact sport. Don't hurt yourself or anything."

Such a smart mouth on this girl.

The urge to silence that smart mouth of hers with his was surprising, but welcome. Yes, kissing her would certainly bring an end to her comments, at least for a little while. He suddenly felt more awake.

"Let's go, brain-dead boy," she said. She walked off in the direction of the checkout counter, leaving him staring after her.

This girl had far too much control over him. Somehow she made him bend to her will and now she was clouding his judgment. Time to take back a little control, starting now.

Chapter Four

They left the boutique a few minutes later with another shopping bag gripped in Gavin's hand and headed down the street. Tali gasped and gaped at the storefronts as they passed, commenting at each window about the treasures she spied inside. Gavin only saw dollar signs—lots of them.

"How about we head back to the hotel for a little while and take a break from shopping?" He tried to sound casual about the idea, but inside he truly hoped she'd say yes. He didn't want to be a whiner, but he wasn't used to pounding the pavement like this for so many hours at a time. Shopping was backbreaking.

Tali paused, her face a fraction of an inch from another windowpane. She trailed her finger down the glass, outlining the necklace displayed on a black velvet background. He peered over her shoulder to get a closer look at what captivated her attention this time. Behind the glass sat a simple necklace, one much simpler than he would have expected to draw her attention.

The piece was beautiful in its simplicity. A modern rectangular pendant hung from a thin silver chain. The pendant was a miniature picture, framed by more silver. Dozens of tiny brush strokes created a scene of…nothing. He couldn't tell what the hell it was supposed to be.

"It's amazing, isn't it?" Tali asked, still gazing at the jewelry.

"Sure it's pretty. I'm not sure what it's supposed to be though."

"That's the point silly. This pendant can be anything to any person. Everyone who looks at this piece will see something different. It's perfect."

Gavin shrugged. "If you say so. Listen, Tali, what do you think about heading back to the hotel for a bit? I'm tired. I could really go for a nap."

"I think you should have worn more comfortable shoes." She laughed and looped her arm through his, steering him down the sidewalk. "Come on, sleepy head. I know the best remedy for jetlag and the cure has nothing to do with a nap in the middle of the afternoon."

She pulled him gently down the sidewalk and he fell into step beside her. He liked the feel of her arm looped through his, her tiny body snuggled up beside him. He wondered what it would be like to stroll along with his arm around her shoulders, but that was a little much for friends, if they could even call each other friends. Looped arms, however, was perfectly acceptable, and surprisingly welcome.

Tali turned a corner and headed off the main road down toward the river. They walked halfway down the block before she stopped to pull open a red door. As they stepped inside, scents of pastries and fresh breads greeted them making his mouth water with unexpected hunger. An espresso machine growled in the corner as the barista foamed milk.

Tali sauntered to the counter. "You're deciding on dinner, so I'm taking it upon myself to choose our snack and rest location. Cool?"

He smiled. There was something so easy about letting her take charge. "Do I have a choice?" he teased, knowing full well he wouldn't put up a fight if she wanted to force him to consume something that tasted as delectable as this placed smelled.

"Nope. But I promise you'll love it."

I'm sure I will.

Gavin stood back and waited patiently as Tali ordered something in French he couldn't pronounce. Her accent was flawless, almost as if she were a native Parisian instead of an American tourist. The way she fit so easily into this world impressed him. She definitely wasn't quite the marshmallow he'd originally thought she was. He wasn't used to having a woman take charge of a situation the way she did. Not that he minded so much right now. On dates, he was usually the one who chose where they ate and what kinds of things they did. Of course this wasn't exactly a date, was it?

Nope. Not a date. So why did his mind go there?

Tali handed him a take-out cup and he gingerly sniffed the liquid inside. The aroma of chocolate and coffee was appealing even though he wasn't really a fancy coffee kind of guy. He usually drank his coffee strong and black.

"Just try the drink, Mr Tough Guy." Tali smiled up at him as if she could read his thoughts. "You're still filled with testosterone if you drink a mocha, no worries. Besides, no place makes a mocha like this place. Anywhere—in the whole world. Trust me, I've looked."

He didn't doubt she had. She was the

kind of girl who could fly around the world trying to find the best mocha available. But was there really anything so wrong with that?

No.

Yes, when you consider all the money she spent on flights could have been used to save gorillas in the Congo. *Since when do I even care about gorillas? Touché.*

Gavin took a sip of the coffee concoction. Damn if the girl wasn't right. Best coffee he could remember having. "This is great."

"I knew you'd like it. Everyone always falls in love with mochas when I bring them here."

"So is this where you bring all your new boyfriends then?"

She grabbed the paper bag from the counter while cocking an eyebrow at him. "Are you my new boyfriend? I must have missed the memo."

"That's not what I meant." Gavin's cheeks burned. Blushing? No damned way. There was no way this girl was going to make him blush. Guys do not blush—certainly not when they're also drinking a mocha.

Yet you blush. Idiot.

"I just—oh, never mind." He sighed and pushed open the door, happy to get back out into the fresh air so maybe he could start thinking straight again. Yes, he'd blame his little faux pas on the sugary smells of the patisserie clouding his otherwise normally clear head.

"This way," she said, ignoring his blaring embarrassment and leading them down toward the river he could now make out beyond a little stretch of park.

They strolled into the park and walked along the path running beside the river until they found an empty bench facing out to the Seine. As they sat, Gavin glanced around the park. Artists stood at easels, carefully capturing the beauty of the scenery around them, each perspective a little different from their neighbor. Gavin was amazed all of the artists could paint in the exact same area and yet each could see something completely different. Sort of the way Tali had spoken about the pendant.

The paper bag in Tali's lap crinkled, bringing his attention back to her. Tali reach into the bag and pulled out two take-out containers of food and a couple of knives and forks. She handed him one set and a container and then opened her own. He followed her lead.

Inside the container was a crepe folded into a triangular packet with its filling spilling out the top. His mouth watered as he cut a bite from the delicacy. Warm creamy berries and nutty chocolate filled his mouth. He sighed and leaned back against the bench, stretching his legs out in front of him. This was the life.

"Agreed." Tali mirrored his posture on the bench as she ate. He hadn't spoken, yet she'd understood his gesture as clearly as if he had said his thoughts out loud. He wasn't sure how to respond to the connection they obviously shared, but he liked it.

He couldn't help but watch her. She'd been nothing but pleasant all day—a stark contrast from their first meeting in the plane while they were over the Atlantic. Today was turning out much better than he'd originally thought it would. Maybe he'd been wrong about Tali after all.

"I'm sorry about yesterday," he said. "I shouldn't have called you those names. I wasn't being fair to you."

"Thanks." She smiled at him, and took a sip of her drink. "But you were at least halfway fair. I am spoiled, but I do try my best not to act like a brat. You happened to catch me on a really bad day and I kind of took my frustration out on you. So I'm sorry, too."

"If you don't mind my asking, what

happened yesterday that made it so bad?"

She set her food down beside her on the bench and took a long sip of her mocha. He watched little lines appear on her forehead as he waited for her to respond.

"Sorry. It's none of my business. I shouldn't have asked." He took another bite of crepe, trying to fill the silence with sounds of eating.

He didn't like to see this new expression on her face. He didn't want her to have to talk about whatever had happened that caused her such obvious pain.

"No it's okay. I need to talk about what happened. I need to deal with everything." She sucked in a deep breath. "I came on this trip alone because I needed to get away from the Meadow for a while."

The Meadow was an elite, gated neighborhood in upstate New York where Tali had lived her whole life. Exactly the kind of place a blue-collar pilot like Gavin would never be welcomed. No, outsiders were never encouraged to become part of the community. Well, maybe someone like Donald Trump would find the welcoming committee on his front doorstep, but no one else ever would.

"What happened?" What could cause her so much pain she would run away all by herself to a foreign country last minute? He'd only been given a few hours' notice before their flight. Just long enough to secure their clearance and submit paperwork for the flight.

"My boyfriend broke up with me."

"Is that all?" He chuckled a little despite his concern for her. A little break up with the boyfriend-du-jour hardly seemed worth this kind of reaction.

"And then I saw him making out with a close friend a couple of hours later."

"Ouch." Okay, maybe that was a little more painful than he'd originally thought.

"Sorry to hear that. Are you sure they were really making out and it wasn't some misunderstanding?"

Tali looked down at her coffee, staring at it so long he wondered if she'd heard his last question. "It wasn't a misunderstanding." She shook her head. "Nope. On the flight, right before I found you at the controls and we—spoke—I went online and found out he's now engaged to my *former* friend."

"So definitely no misunderstanding." He shook his head. The tears from the day before finally made sense—she'd lost not only a boyfriend, but also a friend. That was rough for anyone. And he'd been a total jerk to her.

Good one, jackass.

"Nope. Not unless 'engaged' suddenly has a new meaning I'm not aware of."

He sighed. "I'm sorry. Now I really wish I hadn't been such a jerk to you yesterday."

"Really, it's okay. I shouldn't have been

a—let's call it even and start over, okay?" She peeked up at him, her eyes clearly asking to move on and leave their brief past in the past where it belonged. How could he deny her one little courtesy after learning what she'd just been through?

He nodded. "Sounds good."

Starting over did sound good. The more time he spent around her, the more he wanted to get to know her. Maybe she wasn't exactly the person he thought she was at first glance. Maybe there was more to this girl than he realized.

"Are you done with your manly crepe and mocha yet? 'Cause I still need to hit Louis Vuitton and find a kickass pair of boots before we call it a day. Oh and I need to stop at this little boutique to pick up some clothes for my little cousins. They look so adorable in matching outfits." She stood and threw her empty containers in the trash. "I can't remember the last time my credit card had this much fun in one day."

He sighed. She really was something else. Maybe he was wrong about being wrong about her. Maybe she really was a spoiled brat. Fun to be around and beautiful, but still spoiled.

"What?" she asked, her lip-gloss brush swiping back and forth across her lower lip. The bright cherry color stained her lips, making them shine in the afternoon sunlight.

Does she taste like cherry, too?

He shook his head, trying to dislodge the thoughts suddenly taking up residence in his mind—images of his tongue stroking a path across her lips, plunging into her mouth, tasting her. He rubbed the napkin across his mouth, wiping away the last traces of chocolate. God, he wished that napkin were her skin. Surely her skin would be soft and silky and warm against his mouth. Much better than the scratchy paper napkin.

"What?" she asked again louder, the impatience clear in her tone. "Why are you staring at me? And what was that huge sigh about?"

"Nothing." He forced his unwanted thoughts of Tali to the back of his mind. He would deal with them later, when he had time to figure out exactly what they meant. Later, when he didn't have Tali looking at him with those slightly pouty, sexy lips. "I didn't think we had so much more shopping left to do. I guess your credit card never gets tired, huh?"

"You're not going to start with the whole spoiled thing again are you? Because if you are, I'm going to have to kick your butt with the new boots I plan on buying."

He laughed despite his best effort not to. "No, I'm not going to call you spoiled even though you clearly are. You're perfectly entitled to spend your money any way you see fit."

"Good, then let's get going. Fabulous

boots aren't going to buy themselves."

CHAPTER FIVE

"Oh, look at these," Tali said pulling Gavin into the shop where she'd spotted the most amazing jeans in a window display. Jeans that screamed to be worn by her tomorrow—make that today.

"What now?" Gavin followed her into the store, the weariness more evident in his voice with every passing credit card swipe.

"These." She held up the jeans to show him her prize. Surely he would agree they were worth the—two hundred thirty-five Euros. Really, three hundred dollars American wasn't much for denim this soft and a cut this flattering. If her usual shopping girlfriends where here, they would absolutely agree.

"They're jeans. Can't you buy jeans back in the States when you get home?"

"Not *these* jeans." She walked into a nearby change room and slipped quickly into the jeans. The soft material hugged her in all the right places as she did a squat in front of the mirror. *Not too tight. I don't even need to break these in.*

She opened the change room door and did a little twirl for Gavin.

"How's my cargo looking?" she teased, looking over her shoulder as she wiggled her butt for him. She planned to buy them regardless of what he thought. Still, it was fun to see his initial reaction when she first showed him something new.

"Just as good as it did in your other jeans."

She clucked her tongue at him. What did he know? Her butt looked completely amazing in these new jeans—not nearly as plain and ordinary as before. As she twirled, she caught a glimpse of a stunning blue corset top. It would look unbelievable with these jeans and her new boots.

Tali stopped twirling and skimmed through the corsets until she found the right size. "One more thing."

Gavin groaned behind her as she closed the dressing room door again. "It's always one more thing. You know we've been shopping for hours. Haven't I been a good boy and earned the privilege of dinner yet?"

"Want some grapes and stinky cheese with your whine? Just let me try this on and then we'll go. I promise. This will be the last thing I try on."

"I've heard that a few times already today. I'm not sure I believe you."

Tali pulled off her top and bra and slipped the corset up around her torso. The top was even more stunning than she thought it would be. She quickly adjusted her breasts into the rounded cups and held the edges together behind her back. Now she just needed to tie the laces running along her spine. Impossible.

"Gavin, can I get your help in here for a minute?"

She heard a loud groan and the chair in the waiting room squeaked as he stood. Her door clicked open and Gavin peeked inside the tiny room. His tired eyes instantly lit up at the sight of her reflection in the mirror. Exactly the kind of reaction she hoped an outfit like this would stir in someone. Especially someone as hot as Gavin.

"Can you lace up the back for me? It's a bit tricky to reach."

"Um—sure," he said quietly, taking the edges of the material from her hands. His gaze shifted to her back and she was suddenly aware of the lack of clothing between her skin and his fingers.

Apparently he was aware of her naked flesh too.

His large fingers fumbled with the laces almost letting them slip. She quickly held the top tight against her stomach so it wouldn't fall to the ground. Not that a situation like that would be completely unwelcome with a guy like Gavin, but she'd prefer not to have it happen in a changing room if possible. Her hotel room? Well, that was different.

Why was she so attracted to him?

'Cause he's hot. And fights back. And hot.

"Sorry," he mumbled, taking the laces and pulling them tight across her shoulder blades. "Is that too tight?"

"No, it's fine."

His fingers stopped moving halfway down her back and his gaze found hers in the mirror. The heat radiating out of his expression was enough to make her feel flushed. She'd asked him to help her get the top on, but now she wished he would tear the damn thing off.

She swallowed the lump in her throat unable to shake the feeling he might be thinking the same thing. Tali turned her head to look at Gavin without the aid of the mirror. "Is everything okay? Did the laces get stuck?"

"Everything's fine," he said softly, only breaking his gaze with hers long enough to shift it from her reflection to look directly in her eyes.

She hadn't realized how close he stood behind her until now—his mouth only inches from hers. With the tiniest effort, she could wrap her hand around the back of his neck and bring his tempting mouth to hers. Oh God, she wanted to get a little sample of his mouth.

"I'll just finish tying this," he said, finally looking away.

He focused on her back again and she let out the breath she hadn't even realized she'd been holding. "That should do it." He rubbed his hands along the smooth material, resting them gently on her hips.

The urge to lean back into him so he

could wrap those hands across her stomach was overwhelming. Something looked so right about their reflection in the mirror. Almost as if she were staring at a framed photo as they stood there together. An unexpected ache flared inside her chest. She wanted more than anything to be with someone—to have a future with someone, a real future, not one that would get taken away from her again.

Roger would have a picture with Samantha in the paper soon and it would probably look like this. The thought made her feel a little sick to her stomach.

Tali closed her eyes and willed Roger from her mind. She was with Gavin—at least as a friend—and she wasn't going to let anyone ruin her time with him. Not even Roger and annoying Samantha.

"What do you think?" she asked Gavin's reflection.

He smiled. "You look amazing. And you

should for—" He glanced at the price tag dangling from the bottom hem of the corset and coughed. "How can this possibly cost so much?"

"It's a steal. Look at the craftsmanship."

"This cost more than my hotel room. You realize that, right?"

Tali rolled her eyes. "Of course it does. It's a designer piece." Really? Had this man never shopped before?

Tali pulled the tags carefully off of the jeans and corset top and slipped into her boots. She stuffed the clothes she had been wearing into one of their many shopping bags.

"What are you doing?" Gavin asked, motioning at the tags in Tali's hand. "You're going to pay for those, aren't you?"

"Absolutely. I just figured we had to work pretty hard to get me into this corset, I may as well stay in it for a little while." Tali stopped at a display of watches on her way to the checkout counter. "You should get this." She held up a gorgeous silver watch that would look fantastic on Gavin. She could already imagine him wearing the timepiece while flying at thirty thousand feet.

He glanced at the price tag. Why did he always look at the price first?

"I can't afford that."

She clucked her tongue. "Sure you can. You just need to put it on credit and then pay it off over a couple of months. This watch is totally worth a few extra interest payments."

Gavin took the watch from her hand, his fingers gently brushing against her palm. A rush of sparks danced across her skin, awakening nerve endings that had lain dormant for a long time. The sensation excited her.

"You're something else, Tali." He shook his head and put the watch back on the display and walked away.

"Something else in a good way, right?" She called after him but he walked out the front door of the boutique without answering her. *What the hell is his problem?* It's only a watch. What's the big deal?

Tali quickly paid for her purchases and struggled to gather her heavy bags. He hadn't even carried her bags out for her. Nice.

"What's your problem?" Tali thrust a handful of bags into Gavin's hand. His mood swings were really starting to annoy her. One minute he was friendly, flirty and teasing her, the next he was grouchy and rude. What the hell?

"Nothing. Let's go."

"No, I'm not going anywhere until you tell me what the hell just happened." She put her hand on his arm, stopping him when he tried to walk down the street. His biceps bulged under her fingers and she couldn't help but squeeze him a little tighter.

Gavin turned to face her. He bent down until his face was level with hers, his mouth hovering so close to hers that she could stick out her tongue and lick him. God she wanted to lick him.

But she wouldn't. That wouldn't exactly be appropriate behavior for two friends while walking down the streets of Paris.

"I said it's nothing. Don't worry about it."

Lick him.

She licked her own lips instead, urging her internal voice to shut the hell up. "It is something. You're lying to me."

"You're right, there is something wrong." He stared at her for a long moment, his mouth so close to touching hers, she could practically taste him already. "You promised me dinner of my choice and I'm starving. Let's go eat."

She tried to mutter a response, but her tongue didn't seem to work anymore for anything other than kissing him. How could he think about eating right now? All she could think about was the heat of his body melting into her, warming her right to her core.

"I'll take your answer as a yes. This way." He took her hand in his free one and guided her down the street.

Tali groaned as she sat on the chair in the middle of a crowded restaurant. There was a small bar along one wall of the restaurant, another wall had windows facing out to the busy street so diners could watch the pedestrians pass by. The rest of the place was decorated in dark colors with pictures of grapes and vineyards hanging on the wall.

The decor was all a little tacky in her opinion, but she tried to relax and not share her thoughts since Gavin seemed quite happy to be there. And she was happy to be with Gavin peacefully and not fighting for a few moments.

The last thing she wanted after a long

day of retail therapy was to sit on the world's hardest chairs, shoulder to shoulder with half of Paris, yet here she was. She could think of about a million other places she'd rather be—in bed with Gavin topped her list.

There'd been two almost-kisses already today. She hadn't been able to think clearly since the first in the dressing room, but the second, wonderful almost-kiss on the street had just about put her over the edge. The whole walk to the restaurant, she fought the fog filling her brain. Then when she thought she'd finally gotten her head clear and could hold some semblance of a conversation, or even string together enough words to find out where he was taking her for dinner, she'd look at him and be at a loss for words all over again.

Her mind kept replaying the heat in his eyes as his mouth hovered near hers. She couldn't help but imagine what it would feel like to have the warmth of his hard body molding into hers, his strong hand on the small of her back. She suppressed a groan as the images flittered through her mind again.

Gavin smiled at her from across the table. What was he thinking right now? Was he thinking about their almost-kiss too? Or had their moment of closeness meant nothing to him? Maybe he was used to being so close to women. Maybe that was how he normally spoke to them. She couldn't even remember what they'd said to each other before the almost-kiss moment happened.

She focused her gaze on his lips as he took a sip from his wine glass. She'd never expected to be drinking the Beaujolais nouveau with a pizza, yet here she was—watching the dark red liquid pass over the softest looking lips she could ever hope to have the pleasure of experiencing. Her head swirled and she'd only had a few sips from her glass.

"This place is nice," she said, trying to

think of something to say that wouldn't lead to them fighting again. She wanted to have a nice relaxing meal while she tried to figure out what the hell had happened between them on the street.

"It's one of my favorites. I come here every time I'm in Paris."

"Really? There's so many other great restaurants in the city. Maybe you should try a new one sometime."

He smiled, the little dimple in his cheek appearing again for the first time that day. He must really be happy in a place like this.

She took another sip of her wine while she waited for their pizza and settled back into her chair. She had let him order their dinner since he enjoyed the food here so much. Now she was nervous about what she would be eating. *Better drink more wine.*

"I know there's other places, and I've tried a bunch of them, too. But when I want pizza, there's nowhere better than here. Wait until you try a slice. I bet you'll agree."

She smiled back. There was something about him that made her feel so relaxed and at ease. "I bet you're right."

They sat silently for a few minutes. She enjoyed listening to the chatter of conversations around them. She didn't even mind the silence between them. There was something strangely comforting about it. She usually felt like she constantly had to make small talk with people, but that didn't seem to be true with Gavin.

Of course the longer she sat there staring at him, the more she imagined what it would be like to peel off his clothes and examine the muscles she'd felt underneath his shirt firsthand. Damn.

"So what do you like to do for fun when you're not flying?" The question was the first thing that came to mind to get her thoughts back from the gutter where they were starting to wander.

"All kinds of things. Sometimes I like to go to the movies, sometimes I like to visit the local museums, sometimes I just want to sit and have a drink and people watch. It's different depending on where I am."

"What's your favorite thing to do in Paris?" She was genuinely curious. She wanted to learn more about this man who challenged her like no one else ever had.

"That's a tough call. I have a bunch of things I like to do here. One of which is this." He motioned to the restaurant. "I love to be out among the people of the city, listening to their conversations, watching their mannerisms. Even though I only speak a little of the language, it's amazing how much I can understand just by watching couples together. It's fascinating to try and submerse yourself in another culture, even if it's only for a few days. Even if the language around me is completely unfamiliar."

She hadn't expected an answer like that. She didn't quite know how to respond. "So, no shopping sprees for you?" She tried to make a joke of their afternoon since it was now painfully obvious to her how difficult a day of shopping was for him to do. She'd only wanted company since she wasn't used to being alone in the city. She hadn't intended to trap him into doing something he hated.

She sighed. Had she really cared about whether or not he wanted to be out shopping with her? Hadn't he sort of made his opinion about her shopping clear all day?

Cringing, she set down her wine glass and rested her head in her hand. She was such a spoiled brat that she hadn't been able to see her selfish actions. She hadn't once considered there might be something else Gavin would rather be doing than following her around.

She really had lived up to his opinion of her. No wonder he'd been infuriated by her. She was suddenly embarrassed by her actions.

"I'm so sorry." She spoke quietly, too mortified with her realization to announce it to the tables closest to them.

"What was that? It's loud in here, I didn't quite hear you." Gavin leaned across the table toward her.

She leaned forward and met him halfway. "I'm sorry," she said louder this time. "I shouldn't have forced you to come shopping with me. I just didn't want to go alone, but I should have realized how selfish that was of me. You probably had other things you would have much rather done besides hanging out with me all day in shops."

His expression softened with her words. "It's okay." He put his hand on hers where it rested on the table between them. The warmth of his hand soothed her, made her feel at peace with him. "I know I've been giving you a hard time about shopping, but the day wasn't all terrible."

"It wasn't?"

Gavin squeezed her hand. "Okay, maybe shopping was terrible, but it made you happy and I'm glad I was the one to make you feel that way today after making you cry yesterday. So it's all fine. No worries."

"So if I cry again tonight does that mean you'll go shopping with me again tomorrow? There are a few stores I still wouldn't mind hitting." She was teasing, but she didn't tell him that.

"No way," he said, waving his hands in front of him, but smiling nonetheless. "I'm done shopping. Tears or no tears, you're on your own from now on."

"I promise I'll try my best not to cry on you again."

"Your pizza." A waiter set down a large pizza in the middle of the table.

Tali eyed the concoction suspiciously.

This wasn't like any pizza she'd seen in the States, and the place she usually ate in Paris didn't serve anything looking remotely like this. "What is that?" She scowled at her dinner.

"It's pizza."

"No, that isn't pizza. This thing sort of looks like pizza and it sort of smells like pizza, but where I come from, pizza doesn't have a raw egg jiggling around on top of it."

Her stomach turned at the sight of the egg whites jiggling gently in the middle of the pizza as Gavin took a slice and placed it on her plate. "You don't really expect me to eat this do you?"

He laughed. "Yes, of course. The egg isn't raw, it's just not well-done. It's good." He pushed her plate toward her and then took a slice for himself. "Trust me."

"I don't know you well enough to trust you."

He laughed again, harder this time. "You

said dinner was my choice, so eat it. There's no backing out now." He took a big bite of his pizza and sighed happily. He nodded at her to follow his actions, but she really didn't want to. "Don't make me force you to try a bite."

"I'm going to need more wine," she grumbled, filling her glass.

Chapter Six

Gavin watched as Tali took a tentative bite of her pizza. She was such an interesting girl—frustrating, infuriating and challenging, but also intensely interesting. "How is it?"

"Not as bad as I feared." She swallowed her bite then took a big gulp of wine. "Goes good with the wine."

"I can see that." He laughed. "You better slow down or I'll have to carry you out of here."

"You're the one who felt the need to order wine by the bottle instead of by the glass."

"Sure, blame your drinking habits on me. That's fine."

Time passed easily as they enjoyed their meal together. He was pleasantly surprised they were able to actually share a meal without fighting for a change. He didn't like fighting with her. Bickering back and forth was something that seemed to keep happening despite his best intentions to keep the peace. Finally getting a reprieve from the conflict was nice. Maybe their fighting was behind them and they could move on.

As the waiter cleared away their plates from dinner, Gavin flipped through the dessert menu. "Wanna share something?"

Tali groaned and leaned back in her chair, rubbing a hand over her stomach. "I don't know if I have any room left."

"So the pizza wasn't so terrible after all now was it?" He smirked, knowing he was right and she was going to have to admit it, something he imagined would be a real challenge for a girl like Tali.

"It was good," she grumbled.

"What was that? I couldn't quite hear you over all the noise in here."

Rolling her eyes dramatically, she spoke louder. "You were right. There, I said it. Are you happy now?"

"Yes, I am." He took another look at the dessert menu. "I'm stuffed too. I don't think I have room left for anything else, no matter how good the crème brulee is here."

"Good. Why don't we head back to the hotel? Between the shopping and the bottle of wine, I'm gonna fall asleep right here at the table if we don't leave soon."

"Do you think you're going to be able to walk out of here without making a spectacle of yourself or do I have to carry you out?"

"I make no guarantees. And remember, this is your fault. You're the one who ordered the bottle. It would've been rude to not drink it."

"Whatever you gotta tell yourself, sweetheart." Gavin signed his name on the credit slip and rose from the table, still feeling surefooted. It took more than a glass or two of wine to make him feel the effects of alcohol. But it was still a good thing neither of them was driving tonight. He didn't like to risk it after having any drinks. "Let's get you home."

Gavin grabbed a handful of bags and used his other free hand to help Tali up from the table. She managed to bend over and retrieve her handbag and the other shopping bags without falling over, but she swayed more than once. Getting back to the hotel was going to be interesting.

Gavin held her tightly with his arm around her waist as they wove their way out through the tables to the front door. More than once he saw her almost hit other customers with her shopping bags. Feeling her body so close to his made him feel warm and protective of her.

As they stumbled out onto the sidewalk he breathed the cool night air into his lungs, hoping the crispness of it would help to clear his head. The air didn't really help. Too much wine, too much food and too much of Tali's closeness clouded his mind, making his judgment feel fuzzy.

Tali leaned into his side as they wandered slowly down the sidewalk together. She stumbled a little, not walking nearly as gracefully in her tall boots as she had earlier, but not completely wasted either. Good thing the hotel wasn't far. He held his arm around her snugly, trying to be her anchor.

"Gavin, I think you fed me too much cheap wine at that cheap restaurant." Her words were still clear, but he wasn't so sure the same was true of her thoughts.

"There was nothing wrong with that restaurant. The food was delicious."

She looped her arm around his waist, her head resting against his chest. Whether she needed him for comfort, warmth or stability, he wasn't sure and he certainly didn't much care. The feel of her body pressing up against him felt great regardless of why it was there.

"The food was tasty, I'll give you that much. But I like a place with a little more décor and ambiance."

He shook his head. "Why, Tali? Why do you have to be such a snob about everything? Why can't you enjoy the little things in life instead of worrying about having the best, being the best?"

"There's nothing wrong with having the best. In fact I think you should learn to appreciate the finer things in life."

Gavin pulled open the front door of the hotel and guided her through with his hand on the small of her back. He let his hand linger there as they waited for the elevator to take them to their rooms. As the numbers climbed, he counted to ten in his head. He didn't want to argue with her again, but she pushed his buttons every chance she got.

"Like the watch. You totally should've gotten that watch we saw today."

"Not the watch." He groaned, annoyed she was starting this again with him.

He stepped off the elevator as soon as the doors opened, happy to be free of the tiny space. He could feel his blood pressure rising. Hadn't they only minutes ago shared a nice meal together? Hadn't they been over this already and talked about the same thing enough for one day—for one lifetime?

"What was that groan for?" She turned to him, eying him as if he were a mystery she had to solve.

He stopped out front of her door and dropped the bags he was carrying. Surely, she could take them from there. "Nothing." He turned to leave before they could get into another argument.

"Don't say that." She called after him, teasingly. "It's always something. Just say what's on your mind. I'm a big girl. I can take whatever you're dishing out tonight."

He turned back to her. Why couldn't she drop it? Why couldn't she let it go so he didn't have to say something he didn't really want to say?

"Come on, Gavin. Get it off your chest." Her eyes were half-lidded from the alcohol, but the fire behind them still burned hot. "Mmm, yes, your chest. We wouldn't want anything tarnishing that now would we?"

"You, okay? You're my problem." He cringed. The words hurt him to say, but they were the truth.

"What about me?" she questioned, taking a step toward him. She put her hands on her hips, challenging him.

Why did everything have to turn into a grudge match with this girl? Well he wasn't going to back down this time. He was going to say what was on his mind and then maybe she'd finally get the message.

"Everything. Everything is always about you. Don't you see?"

She sucked in a quick breath. "Why,

because I asked you to go shopping with me?"

"No." Gavin took another step closer, hoping maybe he could get her to actually *listen* to what he said instead of only hearing the words but not the meaning. "Because you don't seem to care or realize not everyone is as rich and materialistic as you are."

"I do realize and care, thank you very much." She straightened her shoulders and stood tall as if she were trying to make herself bigger than she was. She still barely came up to his shoulder, but it was sort of cute that she tried. If only she wasn't so frustrating all the time, he might be able to enjoy her being this close to him. "I thought the watch would look good on you, that's all. Excuse me for trying to add a little style to your otherwise boring wardrobe."

Now she was going to get an earful. No one insulted his wardrobe. That was mean and uncalled for.

Gavin took a step forward, his chest

almost touching hers as he towered over her. "I don't really need your help, but thanks. I'm happy with my boring clothes and my fifty-dollar watch. Unlike you, I don't need to prove my worth with a bunch of fancy trinkets."

Tali jabbed her finger into his chest, poking his breastbone hard with a sharp fingernail. Her touch wasn't all together unpleasant, but he would have enjoyed it more if she were touching him in a slightly different manner. Say a gentle scratch along his ribs with those nails instead. Now he wanted to groan for another reason. The fantasies starting to flood his mind were tempting. Very tempting.

"I am not trying to prove my worth to anyone. You don't know anything about me."

"Don't I?" He edged closer to her, unable to resist the draw of her temper fighting him, pushing him. He wanted to tame her temper. "Don't I know you'll buy whatever you want, spend without considering the cost, and assume everyone else wants to do the same?"

Tali pushed her hand flat against his chest in an attempt to make him step back, but he held his ground and the only thing she succeeded in was finding his pounding heartbeat beneath her hand. She paused for a moment, and he held his breath waiting to see what she'd do next. He didn't have to wait long. She followed the ridges of his toned muscle, her fingertips brushing over the hard ripples of his stomach, sending a wave of electricity through him. He wanted her to keep going until she'd explored everything he had to offer. But she stopped.

"No." She closed her eyes as if she tried to fight feelings she had for him. Possibly the same feelings he was unexpectedly feeling for her. Yet, she let her hand linger where it was, teasing him and torturing his flesh. "No you don't know me at all."

Tali took a deep breath, leveling her gaze on his. She suddenly looked too serious, like she was going into battle. "You think because you spend one day with me you know me, but you don't. Sure I spend a little money, but there's a lot more to me than that. Too bad you're too much of an arrogant asshole to ever find out."

Arrogant? She should talk.

Gavin narrowed his eyes at her, his gaze never straying from hers. "Maybe when you prove to me there's more to you than money, I'll finally believe it."

"Maybe when you finally stop thinking you're hot shit, I'll have the chance to prove there's more to me than you think, but right now I can't seem to get out from behind your giant ego." Tali's chest heaved as she tried to catch her breath.

He watched mesmerized as her breasts fought against the tight corset he'd tied hours early. He suddenly wanted to rip the material from her body to free her of its confines.

Without thinking it through, Gavin crushed his mouth against hers, stealing her breath. He flicked his tongue across her lips and her mouth opened, inviting him in. He tangled his hand in her hair as he explored every crevice of her mouth then gently bit her lower lip.

Tali went limp in his arms and he held her tighter against his body, his hand pressed firmly into the small of her back, holding her to him—every hard inch. He moved against her, pressing her up to the wall beside her door. Even with her every contour melting into his, he still couldn't get close enough to her to satisfy his growing need.

"Damn right I'm hot shit," he muttered still kissing her and loving every second of how she responded to him. "And I plan on proving as much to you right now."

He needed her. Damn it. She could ignite a flame in him so hot they might accidentally set the sheets on fire. That was fine with him. Tonight he was going to tame that smart mouth of hers.

"Gavin," she said into his mouth. "Get the door." She thrust a plastic keycard into his hand.

He broke away from their kiss and slammed the card into the lock, twisting the handle sharply when the light flickered to green. Pushing open the door with one hand, he pulled her through the opening with his other.

"The bags. I can't leave them in the hall."

"You and your stupid bags." He growled not giving a hot damn about the bags, but he bent to grab them, throwing them through the doorway anyway. He didn't want anything to distract them from this moment and if having her shopping bags safely inside would comfort Tali, then by all means, he'd bring the damn things into the room.

"Well I'm not about to leave that kind of merchandise out in the hall for people to take. I might be free with my spending, but I'm not going to throw money away."

"If you say one more thing shopping related, I swear I'll walk out of this room no matter what we're in the middle of. Got it?"

"Got it." She smirked. "So aren't you supposed to be proving to me how hot you are right now? 'Cause so far I'd say you're still just about lukewarm."

"Lukewarm, huh? Is that the best you can come up with?" He knew she was trying to goad him on, but his body responded regardless. Oh, he was going to prove how hot he was all right, even if doing so took all night—even if convincing her took multiple tries.

He let the door slam behind him and eyed Tali. She stood near the bed, her breathing fast as she watched him. He wanted to pounce on her like a cheetah claiming its prey, but he wouldn't. Instead, he would let her sweat out the anticipation for a few moments longer.

Good God, the woman looked so damn hot he could barely stand the reaction she caused inside of him. With her fitted corset top showcasing the rounded mounds of her breasts, the skinny jean hugging her ass, and the knee-high black boots, she could have been some kind of modern day superwoman—her super power being the ability to seduce men with a single eyelash bat.

Gavin moved across the small space between them as if pulled to her by some kind of magnetic force. He looked down at her, fully taking in the view of her breasts peeking out over the top of the corset.

Pulling his gaze back to her eyes, he tucked a strand of hair behind her ear before cupping her jaw with both hands and brushing his lips over hers. Her hands slid across his hips and under the hem of his shirt, heating his skin with her touch. He pushed his tongue past her teeth, anxious to taste her again as he tangled one hand in her long tresses. She arched her back into him in response.

His other hand left her jaw, tracing a line down her neck to her collarbone then followed the path with his mouth. He dragged a fingertip down her chest, dipping it into her deep cleavage then cupping her breast in his hand. Her breasts heaved against his touch, but they were still held captive by the damned corset.

He bent further, kissing the tops of her breasts as he kneaded the soft flesh. He tugged at the edge of the corset, trying to pull the tight material from her body but it wouldn't budge.

It's like a freaking trap.

He spun her around so her back was now facing him. He'd been imagining ripping the corset off of her all evening, never thinking he'd actually get the chance. Now the chance presented itself, he would savor the moment.

Gavin untied the knotted bow at the small of her back and smiled as the edges of the corset came apart a fraction of an inch, widening the gap across her spine. Tugging on one of the strings, the top loosened even more. He knew he could probably get the top to fall to the ground now, but there was something so satisfying about watching the string come free from each little hole. He slid a finger up her spine, hooking his knuckle around one of the crisscrosses and pulling both strings free at once. This was good—faster, yet still teasingly tedious.

When the string pulled free of the last set of holes, the top fluttered to the carpet soundlessly. Her milky white skin was smooth under his fingertips as he rubbed his hands down her back. After a moment, he snaked his hands under her arms, wrapping them around her and cupping her breasts. Tali moaned and leaned back into his embrace. She tilted her head to the side and he kissed the crook of her neck.

He licked a path up to her ear with his tongue while he pushed his hand south, expertly unfastening the button of her jeans. Slipping his fingers beneath the edge of the silken material of her panties, he whispered in her ear. "Still lukewarm?"

Her mouth was on his instantly as his fingers danced over her sensitive flesh. She moaned into his mouth and he resisted the urge to smile with satisfaction at finally proving her wrong.

Tali's head spun as she tangled her tongue with his, tasting him. And it wasn't only because of the half bottle of wine she'd consumed earlier. God, he tasted good. His body felt even better. She leaned into him, her body craving more from him—as much as she could get.

He pulled his mouth from hers and her eyes fluttered open. He was hot. So unbelievably hot. She'd been wrong to tease him about being lukewarm since he was nothing short of smoldering.

"Must you always be such an asshole?" she asked as his hand still touched her in ways she hadn't felt before. She needed to get the hell out of her jeans. "I admit it, you're hot. Lucky for you, good looks go great with your arrogance."

"I think you like my arrogance, because now you finally have someone who can stand up to your hardheadedness."

"Don't start with me." She bit his lower lip and sucked it into her mouth for a moment before speaking again. "Or I might not play nice with you."

Gavin grinned. "Who said anything about playing nice?"

Tali squealed with surprise as he picked her up and tossed her unceremoniously onto the bed. He unzipped her boots and let them fall to the floor with a thud. Grabbing her jeans near the ankles, he gave them a couple of solid tugs and pulled them from her body, throwing them into the corner of the room.

She loved seeing Gavin tower over her, taking control. Normally she was always the one telling people what to do and making decisions. Letting Gavin take control away from her, for a little while, was freeing. He was very good at taking control of a situation.

She lay still on the bed as she watched Gavin pull his shirt over his head and toss it onto the floor. Her eyes travelled down his chest, following the little trail of hair disappearing beneath his jeans. She wanted to see for herself where that hair led. She sat up and reached for him, but he gently pushed her back down to lay prone.

"Stay," he said simply.

She laughed at his forwardness. She liked he wanted to take control, but this seemed like he was getting a little carried away. "I'm not your dog."

"No, you aren't, but you really should listen." He tugged open his pants and slipped out of them and his boxers at the same time. He held them long enough to retrieve a condom from his wallet before dropping his pants to the floor to join his shirt. She giggled as he casually tossed the condom onto the bedside table as if it were his car keys.

He answered her laugh with a devilish smile. "I promise I'll make your obedience worth your while—if you're a good girl."

"What if I'm bad?" she teased.

"I'll make your deviance worth my while."

She didn't know what the hell he meant, but she certainly liked the sound of it. "Well, now I'm confused. Should I be good or bad?"

He climbed onto the bed, kissing his way up her legs. "I think you should shut up and relax for a little while, and let me do what I do best. You talk entirely too much sometimes."

She squirmed as he kissed the inside of her knee. She never knew she was ticklish there but his prickly five o'clock stubble tickled her delicate skin. His kisses fluttered across her skin, awakening nerve endings as he went. "I thought what you did best was fly."

He bit her inner thigh. "Shush, woman. How hard is it to be quiet and enjoy the moment without a running commentary?"

His mouth travelled further along her thigh until he reached the edge of her pink lacy thong. She tried to stay still, but she couldn't help squirming as he slid the smooth material over her hips, pausing only long enough to brush his lips against her skin.

"Didn't I ever mention I'm exceptionally skilled at this?" He dipped his head, finding her eager flesh waiting for him.

Tali groaned loudly, arching her back

while his mouth did things she'd only previously imagined possible. "You totally didn't mention this. I would have remembered." She groaned again from deep inside her chest, giving in completely to the sensations as her muscles clenched with the flood of pleasure taking over her body.

"You should teach a class or something." She gulped in the air as she tried to catch her breath. Hot damn. Did sex get any better than this? How could he possibly top that?

He laughed. "I'll take your suggestion into consideration."

Gavin settled himself between her legs, wrapping them around his waist. He reached for the condom he'd set on the night table and sheathed his length. Gripping her hips with both hands, he lifted her slightly and slowly inched into her heat.

As he moved, she tilted her hips to meet his, deepening every thrust. Her head spun and her dizziness wasn't from the alcohol. She'd been wrong to think the night couldn't get any better. So, so wrong.

Gavin sat back on his heels, dragging her with him so she straddled his lap. She was more than happy to accommodate him. At this point she was game for whatever he wanted. He was so talented—he was probably semi-pro. If there were such a thing.

Tali draped her arms across his shoulders, gripping his back and kissed his neck as he moved inside her. Her body grew tighter with every passing second as he sped up his pace. She threw her head back, giving in to the moment of pure ecstasy as he shuddered inside her then stilled, holding her close.

His breathing was as ragged as hers as they collapsed back onto the bed. She settled into the crook of his arm, resting her head on his chest. Gavin reached for a blanket and pulled it across them as the excitement of the day—and night—finally caught up with her. Her breathing slowed and she tried not to focus on the room spinning around her as she listened to Gavin's pounding heartbeat.

Tali squinted as the bright morning light invaded her senses. They hadn't slept much the night before with all the sexy time happening. At one point they stopped long enough to order burgers from room service to refuel, but then they were back at it. She was exhausted and sated and so unbelievably happy.

Gavin was just about the last person she would have imagined getting together with since she'd never met anyone with a mouth like his. But here she was in bed with him.

Huh. Didn't see that coming.

Since this whole nonsense had happened with Roger, she really hadn't seen herself hooking up with anyone for a while. But she guessed there's no telling what can happen in life or when you'll meet someone who will make you act spontaneously.

Spontaneous had worked out pretty well this time.

She rolled over to find Gavin mysteriously missing from her bed. He'd been here a few hours ago, but then she must have really crashed for the night from complete and utter exhaustion. She glanced toward the bathroom, listening for the shower running, but she was met with silence.

"Gavin?" She called out even though it was obvious he wasn't there to answer her. Where had he gone? And why had he left without so much as a kiss goodbye?

Chapter Seven

Gavin rolled his neck as he waited at the end of the counter for his coffees. The night with Tali had been better than he'd imagined it could be. He hadn't planned on pulling an all-nighter, but being with her was too great to only be a one-time thing. Multiple times had been much more satisfying.

Tali had really surprised him yesterday. He'd gone into shopping thinking it would be terrible, and part of it definitely hadn't been great. But he'd also seen another side of her. She wasn't like the usual rich girls he'd been around who simply looked at a designer label and assumed the name made it good. No.

Tali looked at the material, the craftsmanship and the care going into each of the pieces she'd purchased. He still didn't understand why she did it, but he liked that she seemed to have a little more depth to her spending than he'd expected. And when they'd been in bed together, she'd been unexpectedly sensual and loving. The change from the personality he'd expected of her surprised and thrilled him.

Hell, Tali was fantastic in bed and to spend time with.

"Gavin? Gavin Taylor?"

He turned at the sound of his name and found a tall blonde waving at him from across the small restaurant. Kerry?

Oh no. Not good.

He waved back without much enthusiasm. "Hey, how's it going?"

"It's going great, darlin'. How've you been?"

Her voice sounded as sugary sweet as honey, just like he remembered. She was a southern girl all the way. She would smile in your face and talk sweet to you, but he knew better. He knew the real Kerry would not take kindly to anyone who didn't treat her the way she demanded.

"I've been fine. What are you doing in Paris?"

"Well, this is my new route, darlin'. Who are you with these days? I haven't seen you around as much as I used to. I miss that."

She came to stand in front of him and walked her fingers up his chest, stroking her hand along the length of his shoulder as she fluttered her eyelashes at him.

Really not good.

"I'm not flying commercial anymore. I've gone private now." He took an instinctual step back, distancing himself from her as much as he could with the counter behind him.

"Private. Wow, aren't you moving up in the world. I'm impressed."

She batted her eyelashes at him again, the fake wisps of black hair reminding him vaguely of spider legs. He shivered. "Thanks."

"So how long are you in town for? I'm here for a few days still, so if you're *up* to spending a day in bed, I'm game."

He shook his head, shuddering a little. He'd slept with Kerry a few times in the past, but that was a long time ago. Back when he was still young—and stupid. "You always were so straightforward. I can't."

Kerry stuck out her bottom lip in a fake pout. She reached into her bag and pulled out a crumpled receipt and a pen. "Here's my hotel number. You call me anytime if you have a change of heart, okay?"

Reluctantly he took the piece of paper, vowing to ditch it in the trash on his way out of the store. He had no intentions of ever sleeping with her again, but there was no real reason to be rude and say that to her face. Besides, the chances of running into her again were unlikely at best. "Thanks. I don't think I'll be able to take you up on your offer though."

She grinned. "We'll see. You never know when you'll get some unexpected free time." Kerry stepped closer to him and went up on her toes. She kissed both of his cheeks, lingering a little longer than was European custom then whispered in his ear. "I'll see you around… hopefully."

"So this is where you got to," Tali said, appearing behind Kerry with a not-too happy expression on her face.

Kerry and Tali smiled politely at each other, but Gavin—and most likely everyone else in a one-mile radius—could feel the tension crackling in the air between them. Not good.

"I was grabbing us some coffees. The hotel makes the worst coffee in Paris." Gavin laughed, trying to lighten the mood. "I guess you had the same idea, huh?" He directed his question to Tali, hoping Kerry would take the hint and leave.

Kerry looked back and forth between the

two of them, taking a moment to obviously eye Tali, evaluating every characteristic about her. "Now I understand," she said to Gavin. "But just so we're clear, my offer still stands. I'll see you around, darlin'."

Gavin sighed as Kerry walked out of the coffee shop. Thank God she hadn't stuck around any longer. He wasn't sure how Tali would react to Kerry and her offer, but he guessed there might be yelling involved and perhaps even more tears.

"So that's nice. You have a friend in the city." She smiled sweetly up at him, taking one of the coffees from the counter.

Oh, good. She's not upset.

"Yep, we used to be on the same route together when I was still flying commercial. She's a flight attendant."

"And she kissed you."

Uh-oh.

"On the cheek, as is the custom in

Europe. That's all."

Tali narrowed her eyes at him. And took a sip of her coffee while he waited, holding his breath. He didn't want to go into details about his previous relationship with Kerri. That part of his life was in the past and he wanted to keep it there, but he also wouldn't lie to Tali if she asked him about his relationship with Kerry or any others. Of course if she didn't ask…

"Is whispering in someone's ear and passing little notes also part of the custom here?"

Crap.

"No, but you should know I told her I wasn't interested." He wrapped her in his arms, careful not to spill her coffee and kissed the top of her head. "I have no intention of spending any time doing anything with Kerry. I swear."

"You're sure? She was awfully pretty. And she seemed very into you. Were you guys members of the mile high club or something?"

"Not quite and let's leave it at that, okay? There's really no sense in rehashing an old relationship that means nothing to me now."

"A relationship?" Tali pushed out of his arms. "Wow. I had no idea your relationship was more than a fling. Should I be worried?"

"Not at all. Kerry isn't my type anymore."

"Oh? What is your type then?"

Good question. He thought he knew, but as of last night, he wasn't so sure. Any day previous to this one, jealousy like Tali's right now would have been a real turn off to him. But now… now it gave him a little thrill that she would feel protective and territorial over him.

He smiled and kissed her gently on the lips. The gesture wasn't enough to really stoke the fire, but it did spark the flame. "I have no idea, but I like what I see right now."

She smiled back at him. "You know, I think sex turns you all soft and mushy. If this conversation had happened yesterday, you would have been full of smart-assed remarks."

Gavin reached around Tali and slid his hand down the small of her back until he cupped one butt cheek in his hands, giving it a gentle squeeze. "Great, now I'm busy thinking about your smart ass."

She giggled. "Lame, completely lame. Not at all your usually witty self. That settles it, sex makes you as tame as a little kitten."

"Be nice. Come on. Let's get out of here. We're up early, the sun is shining, birds are chirping their little bird butts off and we're both free to do whatever we want until my bitchy—I mean beautiful—boss tells me it's time to fly her home. So what's on the agenda for today?"

They wandered out onto the empty sidewalk together. The crowds from the night before were probably still sleeping away their shopping exhaustion. That's what they should've been doing too, but once Gavin was up and awake, he could never go back to sleep, no matter how tired he was. He was better off getting up and getting on with his day. Seemed Tali agreed.

They strolled down the sidewalk in silence for a few blocks. Gavin enjoyed learning they could be in each other's company without having to constantly chatter about something. A shared comfortable silence could be really hard to find. Once again, he was surprised he'd found such unexpected qualities in Tali.

Why wasn't she like all the other rich party girls he'd known before her? She wasn't the first girl he'd met from Meadow Ridge, but she certainly didn't act like the others. She seemed so much more thoughtful and inquisitive about things—about everything.

They stopped at a corner, waiting for the light to change so they could cross the street. Down the block the banners for the Musée d'Orsay fluttered in the slight breeze. Gavin checked his watch. The time was shortly after ten, which meant the museum would be open to the public now.

"Want to go in?" he asked, motioning toward the beautiful stone building.

"Absolutely. This is one of my favorite places in Paris."

Really?

How was it that this girl could constantly surprise him? How was it this girl, who'd power-shopped the entire day before, was now content to wander through a museum? She was one big contradiction.

As they meandered through the museum, Tali frequently stopped to closely examine some piece of art or another. One time she stopped at a sculpture of a woman lifting a veil away from her face. Tali looked at the sculpture with such careful consideration, he began to wonder if she could relate to it in some way. Did she feel like she was hiding behind something too? Did she long to be seen like this woman?

Maybe she simply thought the sculpture was pretty.

They stopped next in a room full of paintings of ballet dancers. Tali sighed quietly as she walked around the room examining the artwork. Gavin couldn't help but study her instead of the art hanging on the wall. Sure the paintings were beautiful, but this woman in front of him was the most interesting thing in the museum.

She was so expressive as she gazed at a painting of a little girl in a fluffy tutu. Her eyes narrowed then widened as she scanned the entire painting up close before stepping back and tilting her head to the side. He watched as her fingers stroked her lips as she stood there, lost in her own world.

If he could have taken a picture of that moment, he could have hung the photo on the wall alongside the most famous pictures and it would have stood out as one of the most captivating. Watching her stole his breath.

"You're not looking at the art," she said, finally coming out of her dreamlike state to take note of him.

He smiled. "I am, just not the paintings."

"You can be very charming when you want to be. You know that, right?"

"Of course I do. And I use it to my advantage as often as possible." He took her hand, leading her out of the room and across the hall to a bench before pulling her down to sit with him. She sighed, leaning into his shoulder. His chest grew tight with affection. How was it possible to feel this after only knowing her a short amount of time? How was it possible his opinion of her could change so drastically between when she'd first yelled at him in the cockpit to now, sitting on a bench in the middle of a museum discussing art?

"It feels good to rest. I can't believe

we've been here a couple of hours already." She covered her mouth as she yawned her words. "I think the lack of sleep is starting to catch up to me."

"We can go if you want. I've seen enough art for one day."

"No," she answered quickly. "I want to see the rest."

He nodded and laid his arm across her shoulders. If she wanted to stay, he'd stay too. But first he had a question. "So what's with you and your interest in art? It seems like this stuff all means a hell of a lot more to you than the average person."

She shrugged. "I don't know. I love looking at the brushstrokes, and the colors and the composition. It's fascinating to see what choices the artist made and then try to figure out why. Don't you think?"

He laughed. "I usually think 'huh, that's nice' and then move on. I guess I'm not very artistic."

"Sorry, I know I stare at each of them too long." She ducked her head to look at her hands resting in her lap. "We can go whenever you're ready."

What? Who is this shy girl?

"No, we'll stay. I'm not criticizing you or anything. I'm only trying to understand. I didn't take you for the artistic type."

She stiffened beside him. "Why not? Because I'm too spoiled and self-centered to care about art? Because the only thing someone like me could ever be passionate about is shopping?"

Whoa.

"Well, you have to admit the first impression you put out there in the world isn't as someone who cares deeply about art. Unless of course the art is draped over a model as they strut down the runway or splashed across the pages of your favorite tabloid magazine."

"First impressions can be wrong you know."

"True. And my first impression of you definitely was wrong. But you can't fault me for seeing what you put out there." He stroked his hand across her shoulder, trying to ease the tension causing her shoulders to rise up around her ears. "I'm trying so hard to figure out who you really are, Tali. That's all."

"I'm just me—spoiled, shopaholic, and sometimes artistic with a hearty dose of bitchy when necessary. And just so you know, I do read more than just tabloid magazines. Got it?"

"Got it." He laughed. "So tell me, since you love art so much, do you create any art yourself?"

"Not really. I'm usually so busy I don't have any time to sit and sketch or paint... or even *think* about art." She got up from the bench and pulled Gavin up beside her. "Come on. I've had my fill of art for the day. Let's go."

Gavin followed Tali out of the museum and out onto the street. "Where to now?"

"The river. I never get tired of walking along the Seine."

He walked with her in silence for a while, unsure of what to say. If she wanted to create art, why didn't she make time to do what she was most passionate about? Hell, she was so rich there was no way she actually needed to work. Didn't she have ample time to sit and draw or paint until her heart was content as could be? Surely, if anyone had the ability to make time for their passions in life, it was someone as wealthy as Tali.

They stopped along the pathway and gazed out over the river, watching as one of the many tour boats floated by. He loved to look at the city. He felt so comfortable and familiar with the city after having been here a few times before. Paris was a place he could imagine calling home if the situation was right.

The old stone buildings, the cobblestone roads, the smell of crepes and coffee in the air—all were things he could imagine immersing himself in if he decided to settle down somewhere. Of course, he didn't see that happening anytime soon if he were going to continue as an on-call private pilot for people like Tali and her family.

No, the only way that would happen was if he one day managed to create his own charter company. He'd always loved the idea, but he also knew he had many years of hard work ahead of him before his dream would ever be possible.

What was Tali's dream? Did she have one? Maybe her dream was simply to go on shopping sprees at all the finest designers in all the most famous cities.

He glanced at Tali, expecting she would be taking in the sights of the river and city as he was, but that's not what he found. Instead of paying any attention to the beautiful architecture and scenery, she was watching an artist as he stroked paint across a canvas.

"Why don't you paint, too?" he asked, referring to the painter she was so obviously interested in.

Tali didn't respond. She simply tilted her head and nibbled on her bottom lip. She appeared to be concentrating so deeply she didn't hear him speak. That, or she was ignoring him.

"Earth to Tali." He nudged her arm with his. "Hey, you okay?"

Tali blinked rapidly before turning her eyes on him. "What was that?"

"I tried to talk to you and it was as if you didn't even hear a single word I said."

"Sorry. I guess I got lost in thought watching the artist paint. His brush strokes are amazing. His work should be hanging in a gallery somewhere if it isn't already."

Gavin smiled. Seeing Tali passionate about something made him relaxed and at peace. When she talked about painting, or any art in general, it was as if something inside of her started to glow, radiating out of her through every pore.

"What was it you were trying to talk to me about?" She looked away from the painter and started walking along the pathway again, kicking at loose stones with the tip of her shoes.

"I was curious about why you're not working on any art while you're here. Or maybe why you're not painting as a full-time thing. You seem to love creating art. Seems like everywhere we go, you find something to look at like it's a masterpiece."

"I just like pretty things." She shoved her hands into her coat pockets. "I love painting, but it's a hobby for once in a while when I have free time, which sadly isn't as often as you might think."

"Why not? You had free time enough to drop everything once you got dumped and run off to Paris. How do you not have time to do a little painting?"

"Gee, thanks for that. You can be a real jerk sometimes, you know that?"

"Listen, I didn't mean to be a jerk. I'm just trying to understand. If you love art so much and being creative and seeing the beauty in everything is such a big part of your life, and you're rich, why aren't you doing what you love all the time? I don't understand."

"Just because I'm rich doesn't mean I don't have responsibilities you know. In fact, I think a lot of the time rich people have even more responsibility dumped on them than the average person."

Gavin laughed. He couldn't help it. She was completely ridiculous. There was no way someone as rich as Tali, who had as much time and money at their disposal as they could possibly want, could ever be as stuck down with responsibility as the average person was. She was flat out delusional.

He shook his head. "No way. Nope. You will never convince me that's true."

"That what's true? That I have responsibilities? Does the thought blow your mind so much when you realize maybe I could be like you in some way?"

"No. I know you're a lot like me. Our fiery personalities constantly clashing is simply one example. I can't see why you aren't doing what you love to do when you have the resources to do whatever you want to do whenever you want to do it."

Tali sighed. "Because I don't have that. Believe it or not, I don't get to do whatever I want, whenever I want. There are things expected of me because of who I am. And those are things I can't ignore, no matter how much I might want to."

"Like what? I'm trying really hard to understand, but I don't get it. You have so much more freedom than everyone else from the everyday bullshit of life."

Tali stopped walking and stood with her hands folded across her chest. "Freedom, huh? Freedom like being forced to take four years of business school I had no desire to take in the first place. Like having to maintain a 3.8 GPA so as not to disgrace the family. Or, how about the fact I'm now being 'groomed' to run the family business one day even though I feel like pulling out my eyelashes one at a time every single day I'm forced to go in to the office."

"What is your family's business involved with exactly?"

"Global marketing and logistics for exporting and importing sustainable products."

"Wow. That's a mouthful. Is the work interesting?"

"Not really. It's important work, but I

can't seem to get excited about doing everything the job entails. I sit in meetings discussing things. A lot."

Gavin swallowed. Well, that didn't sound as luxurious of a lifestyle as he'd imagined her having. Maybe her life wasn't all fun and games and shopping trips. But couldn't she still make her own decisions about things?

"Okay, so it's not all shopping and fancy dinners, but don't you still get to have a mind of your own? Don't you still get any say in your life and how you spend your time?"

"Sure, I can say whatever I want. And maybe if I had some siblings, I'd be able to do whatever I want too. But I'm the only Radcliff child in line to take over when my father is ready to retire. There's no way he'd ever sell the business and he would never leave the company to someone who wasn't his own flesh and blood."

There had to be a way for Tali to do

what she loved and what she was obligated to do, too. Couldn't there be a balance?

"Can't you work at the business part time and do your art the rest of the time?"

"You don't understand, Gavin. Let it go."

"No. You need to stand up for yourself and do what makes you happy instead of what everyone else wants you to do. You have no reason not to. Tell your family the truth about how you feel and I'm sure they'll understand."

"No, they won't. I don't have one of those television show families where everyone understands and everything is perfectly peachy in thirty minutes. Back off about it already."

Gavin thought back to all the shopping they'd done the day before and suddenly Tali's love for fashion made perfect sense. She hadn't been looking at those clothes as an impulse buy, she looked at them with respect for the artist who had created them. Art was her dream, her passion—she had to do it.

He couldn't even imagine what his life would be like if he wasn't allowed to do the thing he was most passionate about—flying. If he were forced to sit in stuffy meetings all day, it would be utter torture. Is that how Tali felt every day?

Rubbing his hands up and down Tali's arms, he tried to comfort her, tried to make her understand he had her best interests in mind. "Just do what you love and everything else will fall into place once you're actually happy."

"Who said I'm not happy?" She challenged, getting right in his face. So close to him that if he really wanted, he could kiss her without much effort. She was pretty hot when she was all hot-tempered.

"You did." He laughed. He couldn't help it. Damn she was strong-willed. She didn't make anything easy, ever.

"I did not. I said I have obligations. I guess a free spirit like you doesn't know what it means to have obligations to anyone other than yourself. And don't you dare laugh at me. My life, my problems, are not a joke."

"I never said they were. But it's about time you stopped acting like some poor tortured soul and realize you are in a position to take your own life in your hands. You whine, but you really have no reason to."

"You need to stop making assumptions about things you know nothing about." She shook her head and Gavin could see tears pooling in her eyes. "I don't know what I was thinking last night. I really must have had too much wine with that peasant dinner you forced me to eat. I can't believe I would let myself be with someone who is so clueless about what life is really like."

"Don't blame last night on the alcohol. And don't you dare imply I took advantage of you. You loved what we did last night. Seems like you have trouble admitting how you really feel about everything. Maybe you should stop pretending for a change and be who you really are for once—stop hiding and blaming everyone else for your place in life and maybe you'd finally let yourself be happy."

Tali wiped away a tear with the back of her hand. Damn. His chest constricted at the sight of the lonely tear and the knowledge he was the reason it was there. Why did he always say things to make her cry?

"I'm sorry," he started, pulling her into a tight embrace. "I shouldn't have said that."

Tali stiffened in his arms. "Get your hands off of me."

He peered down at her, not loosening his grip. "Tali, really—I'm sorry. That was uncalled for and I didn't mean to make you cry again."

Tali's hand ran up against his chest and pushed hard against him. "I said let go of me." She spoke through a clenched jaw and he could tell she fought to remain in control of her emotions. Reluctantly, he let her go.

"Tali, I—" Gavin stopped mid-sentence as the sting of her hand slapping his face surprised him. His cheek tingled as he stood there staring at her, unblinking.

Did she really just hit me?

"You hit me." He rubbed his newly tender skin. *She hit me.*

"You, Gavin Taylor, are the biggest asshole I've ever had the misfortune of meeting. You do not and will not ever understand me or the life I'm forced to live. Being with you was a mistake, but not because of the alcohol—because you're an ass and I can do a hell of a lot better than you. So why don't you go find that airline whore who obviously wanted to be in your company and go insult her for a while—because I'm done with you."

Ouch.

"Tali, wait," he called after her as she stormed down the path. He jogged up behind her, putting his hand on her shoulder.

"Get your hand off of me before I break your fingers." She glared at him from over her shoulder and he instantly dropped his hand to his side.

"All of a sudden I'm not good enough for you anymore, huh? Not now that I'm saying something you don't want to hear. Well fine then. Run off and find someone new who will listen and nod at whatever Princess Tali has to say. Good luck. That tactic really seems to be working out great for you so far."

"Fuck you, Gavin." Tali took off across the grass, ignoring the pathway all together and made a beeline for the street. She flagged down a taxi and hopped inside before he could even mutter a reply.

"Well, damn. I didn't see that coming."

As he watched her taxi pull away from the curb, he sank to the ground and put his head in his hands. *What the hell just happened?*

Chapter Eight

Tali swiped at the tears on her cheeks with a balled up tissue. She took a few deep steadying breaths and rested her head on the back of the torn leather seat, closing her eyes. What happened back there?

She liked Gavin. A lot. More than she cared to admit to him or even herself for that matter. But why did he have to be such an asshole all the time? Why couldn't he take her word for how her life was and leave it at that? Why the hell did he have to challenge every single thing she said?

God, he was so incredibly frustrating. She wanted to punch him. Instead she'd slapped him. Not smart. Not fair either. But totally justified in that one moment. And satisfying. Oh God, so satisfying.

The expression of shock mixed with a little bit of amusement on his face as the red mark appeared on his cheek from her slapping him was something she wasn't going to forget anytime soon. Nope. That was going into the vault for safekeeping just in case she ever wanted to relive it again.

Tali handed the driver a few bills as he pulled to a stop at the curb. She climbed out of the taxi, thankful she didn't have a ton of shopping bags to lug with her this time. Today she wasn't in the mood for shopping. No, today she wanted to sit and think for a bit. She pulled open the large, heavy door and stepped inside an exquisitely decorated lobby.

Tapestries hung over top of rich amber-colored walls. Oil paintings sat on easels along the edges of the room, giving it the feel of a gallery instead of a restaurant. The whole room smelled slightly of something similar to honey. Tali instantly felt at home.

"*Bonjour, Mademoiselle Tali. Comment ça va?*" The maitre d' sauntered over to her, giving her a quick kiss on each cheek.

"I am well. How are you, Henri?" Her chest swelled a little as if she spoke to an old friend.

"I am very good. You are looking a little tired, *non*? You have been missing your favorite food, *oui*?"

"*Bien sûr.* I haven't been able to stop thinking about the amazing food here since I arrived. Do you have a spot out on the terrace for me today, Henri?"

He smiled sweetly at her. She knew he would do whatever needed to get her the table she desired. And he knew exactly which table she wanted without her having to tell him. Having people remember her likes and dislikes was definitely one of the perks of being a Radcliff. Doors magically opened for Tali. Well, not all doors. Some were still firmly closed—like the door that would allow her to walk away from being forced to take over the helm of the family business. That door had no key to unlock it.

Henri led her out to the terrace to the small corner table she loved so much. Her favorite spot on the terrace had not only an outstanding view of the city, but the table was also slightly removed from the others. She always felt like she was a little bit alone when she sat there, no matter how crowded the restaurant got. Right now, that was exactly what she needed—some time alone with her thoughts.

Tali ordered coq au vin, her favorite meal, and relaxed back into the cushy chair. These chairs were much more luxurious than a person would expect to see on an outdoor terrace, but Tali appreciated the comfort they provided. She imagined they must bring them in each night to prevent them from getting ruined by the weather. Good thing they did. These chairs were far too nice to let something like the elements touch them.

She took a small leather-bound case from her handbag, opening it in her lap. She always carried the sketchbook with her since she never knew when she'd be able to sneak in a few minutes to draw. As she flipped the pages, she remembered where she'd been when each drawing had been created. Some of the sketches she'd done while waiting for her father to start a meeting. Those ones were usually small and always incomplete. Then there were other drawings that were full page, detailed pieces of art. She knew she should probably take them out of the sketchbook and put them somewhere safer where there wasn't a chance for them to get wrecked, but there was something comforting about having them near her. And even when she didn't have time to draw something new, she still enjoyed looking over her previous work.

She stopped flipping as she came to a page she'd done the other day on her flight to

Paris—a picture of a man down on one knee holding her hand and gazing at her with more love in his eyes than she'd ever seen in real life. The day she'd drawn this was the day she'd found out Roger was getting married and her own hope for the future had been crushed. She dreamed of getting married to a wonderful man one day, but with every stinky relationship, or lack of relationship, her dream seemed to move further and further out of the realm of possibilities.

Tali scowled as she examined the would-be groom's face. She hadn't purposely been sketching anyone in particular. She had only been trying to pass the time. But now that she really looked at what she'd drawn, it was obvious—the man in her sketch was Gavin. She'd started this drawing after her encounter with him in the cockpit and he must have still been on her mind. There was no mistaking his telltale five o'clock shadow.

Damn it. Of course, she had to have a crush on the guy who was a total jerk to her all the time. *Just a glutton for punishment, aren't you?*

She traced the lines of the drawing, remembering what it was like when she'd run her fingers down his chest. She could still feel his warm flesh under her fingertips. She could see his dark eyes gazing at her hungrily, reflecting her own need. That handsome face of his—ugh, she'd slapped that handsome face.

Why had she slapped him? Why had she told him off and walked away from him?

Because he'd been a jerk.

True. But he'd also been right.

And what had she done in response? She'd run away from the truth, sulking like a spoiled brat. Tali looked down at her designer boots, her designer handbag still sitting on the chair next to her—her wrists adorned with baubles and sparkly trinkets. She cringed.

She forced herself to think about going back to the States and sitting in a stuffy boardroom with her father, listening to him chatter on about facts and figures and pointing at graphs on the wall. Her stomach twisted into a tight knot. She could almost smell the coffee and donuts in the air as she imagined being forced to sit for hours in the meetings she cared nothing about.

Gavin was right. She would never be happy doing something she felt forced to do. She'd never learn to love the boardroom like her father did. But what could she do about it? Her father needed someone to take over the business one day and that someone was supposed to be her. What would happen if she said no?

What would happen if she said yes? Would her father really want her to run his company, if she hated working there? Wouldn't he want someone who loved the job to run the company he'd created and poured his blood, sweat and tears into for years?

Wouldn't her father ultimately want her to be happy?

Tali sighed and glanced back down to the sketchbook still open in her lap. She wasn't sure she knew the answers, but she had to hope her father would want her to be happy regardless of whether or not she took over for him.

She flipped to a clean page and slipped the charcoal pencil out of the sleeve. She began sketching the scene of the terrace restaurant—the tables and chairs, the ivy climbing the walls and the city backdrop. Instantly the feeling of dread twisting in her stomach disappeared. A feeling of calm seeped in as if she were completely submersed in a tranquil pool.

She added in another detail to her sketch—a man, leaning on the edge of the stone railing bordering the terrace. Not just any man. Gavin.

My Gavin.

Closing the sketchbook and sliding it into her handbag, Tali pulled out a few Euros and tossed them on the table. As she quickly gathered her things, her mind began to clear. She knew what she needed to do. She needed to talk to Gavin.

Tali hurried along the sidewalk, nearing the hotel with every step. Hopefully Gavin was in his room and she could talk to him. Tell him he'd been right about her and she was going to talk to her father about the job he expected—but never asked—her to do. Then she would make things right with Gavin so maybe they could spend a little more time together since she couldn't seem to stop thinking about him.

She picked up her pace, eager to get to him, even more eager for the chance to make up with him. She smiled at the thought of what making up could entail. Hopefully sexy time would be involved. Lots and lots of sexy time.

Tali stumbled, falling forward, landing on the sidewalk on her hands and knees. Her ankle screamed at her as it was held in an awkward position. She carefully pulled her foot free from where her spindly heel had gotten caught in a deep crack in the sidewalk. Trying not to twist it, she stood, brushing the dirt off her pants.

Balancing her weight on her other foot, she put one hand flat against the window of the building beside her and gently rolled her ankle with the other hand. Aside from a slight twinge of pain, it felt okay. By tomorrow it would be good as new again as long as she got back to the hotel and out of the heels soon.

She tentatively put weight on her foot, taking a moment to make sure her ankle would bear weight like normal. She sighed with relief as she took a tiny step and didn't have any pain. Good. No harm done—other than looking like an idiot. Tali glance around her, thankful the sidewalk was empty which meant no one had witnessed her little mishap.

Then Tali's gaze fell to the coffee shop window her hand was currently pressed against. It was the same shop she'd been to earlier with Gavin. Inside, a few patrons had big silly grins on their faces as they watched her. Maybe her little fall wasn't as invisible as she'd originally thought. But it wasn't those people who caught her attention. Nope. Her attention fell fully on one person—Gavin.

Well, make that two people—Kerry, sky whore extraordinaire, was with him.

Tali stood frozen to the sidewalk as she stared through the window at Gavin. He was cuddled up nice and cozy in a cushy booth with Kerry. *Don't waste any time, do you?* Kerry had her head nuzzled into his chest and his arms were wrapped tightly around her. As Tali watched, Gavin kissed the top of Kerry's head.

Huh. Hadn't he done that to Tali too? Hadn't he held her the exact same way before?

Tali's pulse quickened as she stood there, unable to look away. Her breathing came in short gasps as she choked back the tears threatening her eyes yet again. God, what the hell was with her and the crying? She never cried and now it seemed like every time she turned around, she was on the verge of crying like a little baby.

Maybe because she kept getting hurt by people she thought cared about her. Well no more. No more tears for Roger… or for Gavin. She was done. She didn't need a man in her life to be happy. She'd figure out happiness all on her own.

Tali took her hand off the glass and smiled weakly at the people still watching her. Then she turned away from them and crossed the street, narrowly missing a Vespa scooter as it zipped down the street. She didn't stop to think, she just moved, one foot in front of the other as quickly as she could. She needed nothing more in that moment than to get as far away from the coffee shop as she could—as far away from Gavin as possible.

Tali didn't stop until she reached her hotel room. Letting the door close behind her, she rested back against it with her eyes closed. She desperately tried to block out the noise of the thoughts running through her head. She didn't want to question what she saw. She didn't want to question what she felt. She wanted to escape it all for a little while.

She needed a little time to sort out everything that had happened in the last couple of days—Gavin, her realization about art and work, all of it. And she needed some time alone to do that.

"Hi, Tali," a familiar voice said amidst the darkness of her still-closed eyes.

She shrieked as her heartbeat jumped

into her throat at the unexpected company. Her eyes popped open for an instant to confirm her suspicion was correct, then slammed shut again as if doing so could make what she'd just seen untrue.

Please don't be true. Please don't be true.

Tali let her head fall back and bang against the door. "Ouch."

"You okay, baby?"

"No. No I'm not okay." She laughed loudly, longer than was appropriate. "I'm so totally not okay."

Tali opened her eyes and leveled her stare on the man who'd apparently thought it was okay to break into someone's hotel room and make themselves comfortable on the comfy bed. Not cool. That he'd also had to nerve to break into the mini bar and steal the one jar of salted cashews, which he knew were her favorite, was simply going too far. No one stole her cashews, especially not him.

"How did you find me, Roger?"

What was he, a spy or something? Did he have agents working for him, keeping tabs on her? Or was he really just a giant pain, destined to make her life miserable and annoying? She guessed the later was true.

"This is where you always stay. Once I knew you were in Paris, it wasn't hard to track you down. And everyone here knows me, knows we're together, so they didn't mind letting me into our room."

She shook her head. "My room and we're not together. I can't believe you. What the hell are you doing here? You broke up with me, remember?"

She crossed the room, grabbing the almost-empty jar of cashews out of his hand and stood beside the bed, glaring at him and wishing daggers would shoot out of her eyes and directly between his legs.

One for each nut. Cashews not included.

His eyes flickered between the jar of nuts and her cold expression. A grin slowly spread across his face. Damn, she wanted to wipe that grin off his face. For many reasons, only one of which had to do with the whole "breaking up with her and immediately getting engaged to her friend" thing.

"I wanted to talk to you and you haven't been taking my calls. Or my emails. Or my texts."

"Yeah," she started, popping a nut into her mouth and crushing it between her teeth. Oh that felt so good. She could crush nuts all night. "Did you ever think maybe, just maybe I did that on purpose? Maybe I didn't want to talk to you after what you did so I ignored you."

"Well," he looked down sheepishly, "I guess I didn't really think about that. Anyway, when I couldn't get a hold of you, I decided to stop in to see your dad to make sure you were okay and he told me you'd run away to Paris."

"I didn't run away... Well, that's not entirely true. I didn't have any reason to stay in the Meadow so I decided to take a little trip to recharge. I wanted to be alone." She paused for a moment, hoping to let that point sink in to his thick skull. "So you tracked me down and followed me to Paris why, exactly?"

Roger sat up and swung his legs around the edge of the bed so he faced her. She took a step back. "I really wanted to talk to you. I know what I did was shitty, and I'm sorry."

For half a second, she almost wanted to believe him. Almost.

"Really? You're sorry you dumped me. Or you're sorry you announced your engagement to Samantha-frickin'-Swanson the next day. Or maybe you're sorry that because of your announcement, I figured out you two were obviously sleeping around behind my back while we were still dating. What exactly are you sorry for?"

She wasn't going to let him get away with this. There was no way he was using his usual nice guy charm and talking his way out of this heap of shit he currently found himself in. No. Frickin'. Way.

He scratched his nails across his forehead and peeked up at her from beneath his hand. "I'm sorry for all of it. Samantha was a mistake. The whole engagement thing was a huge, ginormous mistake of epic proportions."

"You bet it was." She threw the empty jar of cashews into the garbage and grabbed a bottle of water from the fridge. She took a few big gulps of the cold water, washing away the salty taste in her mouth. It was almost as if she were washing away her feelings about Roger, too.

Seeing him now, she knew she'd been wrong to think he might be the one. Sure, he had a few of the qualities she wanted in the guy she'd spend the rest of her life with, like good looks, a stable bank account, and aspirations for more in the future. But the things she really wanted the most—respect, to be loved unconditionally, to be supported emotionally—those were never things Roger would ever be able to give her. Never. It wasn't in his blood.

"I want you back, babe. I broke it off with Samantha and I want you. I was wrong to ever let you get away, but I'm willing to make it up to you."

She laughed again. "Make it up to me. That's a good one. Like all of a sudden, you're going to say something or do something that will magically repair the broken heart you inflicted on me. Yeah. Good luck."

Tali stepped back again as Roger stood from the bed and approached her. He stroked his hand along her jaw and she jerked her head away from him. His touch was like being rubbed with poison ivy—it made her skin itch.

He dropped his hand to her shoulder instead and gripped her tightly.

"Give me a chance to prove to you how sorry I am and I'm sure we can find a way to work this all out."

"No. I don't want to work anything out with you. Hell, I flew across the Atlantic to get away from you. What part of that tells you I would want to get back together with you? We're over. Whether or not you screwed up things with Samantha is your problem, not mine. I'm done with you."

"You aren't." He pulled her against his chest and wrapped his arm tightly around her lower back.

She arched her back away from him, but his hold on her was strong. Too strong. "Let go of me." She tried to sound as strong and forceful as she could.

"Give me a chance and you'll remember how good we are together. One kiss, baby.

That's all I need."

"No. Let go of me right now." She struggled against him, straining her body to break free of his hold. When the hell did Roger get this strong?

Roger wrapped his hand around the back of her neck and held tight so she couldn't turn her head away from him. Crushing his mouth to hers, he forced his tongue past her lips and into her mouth. The smell of his after-shave filled her nose and the familiar scent suddenly made her feel nauseous. He groaned into her mouth. Her heartbeat pounded in her throat and her breath hitched. She had to get away.

She did the only thing she could think of—she bit down hard on his tongue. He pulled back from her quickly and she jerked her knee up, catching him right between the thighs. Bull's-eye.

Roger dropped to his knees, mumbling something incoherent on the way to the floor.

Tali stumbled backward, bumping into the bed and falling down to sit on the edge of the mattress. She never took her eyes off Roger.

"What was that for?" he asked, finally getting out words that actually sounded like words and not garbled noises.

"Um, because you forced yourself on me." He had to be kidding, right? He had to know what he'd done to her was wrong.

"I wasn't forcing myself on you. I was proving to you that you still have feelings for me." He struggled to his feet and gripped the edge of the bedside table while he stood straight.

"The only lingering feeling I have for you is the pain in my knee from where it collided with your brain. And I'll do it again in a heartbeat if you ever try a stunt like that again."

She was leery of him and ready to bolt for the door the second he even looked like he might attempt another kiss. Roger took a step toward her and she flinched.

"Relax," he said, raising his hands defensively. "I've got it. I won't touch you again."

Roger crossed the room and sat cautiously in the wooden chair in the corner, groaning as he changed positions. Tali couldn't help but smile a little on the inside at his obvious discomfort. After putting his hands—and lips—on her the way he had, she wanted him to have a reminder of why forcing himself on her was such a stupid thing to do.

"Why are you really here, Roger?"

He sighed. "I made a mistake with Samantha. She's making all these crazy wedding plans already. I'm going to go broke on the ceremony alone, not to mention the honeymoon she's planning for us. I can't do it. I can't deal with her. I should have stayed with you."

"Gee, thanks for your heartfelt declaration of your love for me, but I'm not interested. If you've made a mistake getting mixed up with Samantha, that's your problem and I'm not going to help you fix it or take you back. It's time for you to leave."

"Why can't you give me another chance? Why do you have to be such a bitch about this?"

She laughed. "Did you hear yourself? Yep. I'm done. Get the hell out of my room before I call security and have you thrown out."

Roger rose from the chair. "You're going to regret this decision when you're old and still alone."

"I think I'll manage just fine, thanks. Now get out." She held open the door, a clear invitation for him to leave.

He passed through the open doorway, but stopped with his hand on the frame, staring at her intently. "What we had was great. We could be great together again."

"What we had was a lie. You were with her behind my back. I'm a lot smarter now and

I'm not about to fall for your shit again." She closed the door behind Roger, barely waiting for his hand to be free of the doorframe.

Goodbye and good riddance.

Chapter Nine

Gavin stood from the booth in the little coffee shop and stretched. He'd been there for a long time with Kerry, talking and rehashing stories of when they'd flown together previously. And when she'd told him about her most recent messy break up, his heart broke at how badly she'd been treated. But there was only so long he could sit there and comfort her. The truth was, he couldn't stop thinking about Tali and worrying about whether or not *she* was okay.

In his time spent with Kerry, he learned he was absolutely and completely over the whole jet-setting lifestyle. Obviously, he still wanted to fly, but he also wanted to have a home base. He wanted roots somewhere with someone special and he knew exactly who he wanted that person to be—Tali.

"Listen, Kerry. It's been great seeing you

again, but I really should run."

Kerry grabbed her coat and handbag and followed him out of the shop and onto the sidewalk that was now crowded with people heading home after work.

"I understand," she said. "It's that girl you were with earlier, isn't it?"

Gavin nodded. "It is."

He didn't know how he would work things out with Tali, but he knew he had to find a way. He hated she'd left upset with him. He hated even more that he'd deserved getting slapped. He rubbed his hand along his cheek, remembering the sting of his skin as her hand connected with his face and smiled.

"Boy, she's really done a number on you. I can't remember ever seeing that expression on your face before." Kerry fastened the buttons on her coat and shouldered her handbag. "You better go fix whatever it is you've done wrong before she gets away."

"How did you know?"

"It's pretty clear you've been distracted this whole time. It just took me this long to figure out why. It was nice catching up with you. Good luck getting your girl back."

"Thanks. I think I'm going to need it."

"She must be something else to get you all worked up this way."

"She certainly is something else," he said as Kerry walked away, leaving him standing on the street alone.

The question now, was how to get her back. She probably wasn't going to want to talk to him after all the things he'd said to her. And he really couldn't blame her. It was her business how she wanted to spend her life. Who was he to tell her what she should or shouldn't do after knowing her for such a short amount of time?

He'd screwed up and now he had to find a way to fix it. He'd never met a girl like Tali before and he wasn't about to let her go. How could he prove to her he would be with her no matter what choices she made, as long as she chose to be with him?

He had an idea. He didn't know if it would work or not. It wasn't as grand and elaborate as other men might come up with, but it seemed right. No, it felt right. Now he had to pray he could make it happen.

Gavin let himself into his hotel room. The hallways were quiet with everyone in their rooms for the night or still out partying. When he'd walked by Tali's room, it had been quiet. He could only assume at this hour she was already in bed, sleeping and hopefully she wasn't out partying with anyone else. He wasn't sure what he'd do if she was. Best to assume she was in her room and leave it at that. Any other way of thinking was sure to lead to him not sleeping, and that's not what he needed.

Not when he had big plans for the

following day to speak to Tali.

As it was, sleeping would be challenging. How could he possibly expect to get a good night's sleep when he would be going over his plans in his head? Who needs sleep anyway?

He took one more peek at the package he'd picked up earlier in the evening before carefully setting it on the dresser for safekeeping until tomorrow. He hoped the gesture would be enough, but only time would tell. And somehow he had to find a way to convince her to see him again. But how?

Tali leaned back against the pillows, the television lighting the darkened room. She flipped channels endlessly trying to find anything watchable, but in the middle of the night in Paris, the local programming left a lot to be desired.

She wasn't really watching it anyway.

No. She was simply lying there in the dark, enjoying the peace and quiet after what had turned out to be a fairly stressful escape to Paris. She hadn't gotten much time to relax and recoup, but at least she accomplished the most important thing on her list—get over Roger.

He was one hundred percent out of her heart and mind. She had no room for him anymore. He would never be able to hurt her again.

Gavin, on the other hand, was a different story entirely. In the few days she'd known him, he'd managed to root himself into her heart, her mind, her entire being so fully she couldn't imagine how she would breathe if he wasn't a part of her life. That's why she had to get him back tomorrow.

Sure, there was the little problem of that girl Kerry to deal with. Gavin must have gone to her because Tali had yelled at him, right? They'd been in the coffee shop, not a hotel room. He'd said Kerry was his past. He had to still feel that way. One little fight with Tali wouldn't make him change his mind, would it?

Tomorrow, she'd find a way to make him listen to her long enough to make things right, even if she had to beg him. Then they could be together in Paris for a little while before she had to go back to the States. He would take her back. She wouldn't give him any other choice but to make up with her.

Besides, once he knew the truth of how she felt, he'd want to be with her. Easy. Problem solved.

Tali startled out of her thoughts as her cell phone came to life on the nightstand beside the bed. The front display lit up and the phone vibrated, rattling noisily against the wood.

"Dad?" she asked into the phone.

How strange for her father to call her knowing how late it was in Paris. Her father always had an uncanny ability to know what time it was anywhere in the world without having to look up the time change or do the math. Probably all those years traveling when he was getting the company up and running, and solidly on its global feet.

Was it some strange coincidence her father would call out of the blue right after she'd made up her mind to tell him she wasn't going to work at the company anymore? The timing couldn't be more perfect. She could tell him now, get the awkward conversation out of the way then talk to Gavin tomorrow.

Gavin would be so proud of her for finally standing up for what she really wanted.

"Hey, honey. Did I wake you? I know it's late there." Her father's voice sounded shaky on the other end of the line. Her father was always even-keeled, not rattled by anything. She'd never heard him lose the calm, cool edge in his voice. Never. This wasn't an average phone call to check on her.

"Dad, is everything okay? You sound funny." She tried to keep her own voice calm. She didn't like hearing that tone in her father's voice.

"I'm afraid not. Stanley had a massive heart attack today on the golf course and it's not looking good for him right now."

"That's awful. Poor Rachelle, she must be so worried." His business partner's wife was one of the nicest women in the Meadow. She was always the first one to lend a hand when anyone needed anything.

"We're all worried." He father sighed. "So listen. I know you're getting over Roger and everything, but I need you to come home now. This is what we've been training you for. I need you to come home and start working in Stanley's place as soon as possible."

Tali's head swam and she wiped her sweaty palms on the bed sheets beside her. Now the moment had come to tell her father what she really wanted and she didn't know if she'd be able to find the words. How could she tell him she didn't want the job?

"I—um." She cleared her throat and tried to focus on what she really wanted and not what other people wanted for her. "I wasn't planning on coming back to work."

"You what?"

Tali swallowed. "I was thinking I might stay here for a while and paint. You know how I've always wanted to do that."

"Tali, this isn't the time to be messing around with some foolish dream. You've had your fun and a chance to get over Roger and now it's time to come home and do your job."

Tali's heart sank into her stomach. Of course he didn't understand. Why had she ever thought he would? Being an artist wasn't something her father would ever accept of her. But it wasn't his choice to make. It was hers.

"But I don't want the job. Didn't you

hear me? I don't want to run the company. I want to paint and sketch and create masterpieces."

"Now you listen to me. I did not raise you to run off and throw away your responsibilities. You've gone to college for this. You've trained for this moment. I'm not going to let you walk away from everything we've been working toward because you're having a little tantrum over Roger. Suck it up and get back here tomorrow. I'll expect to see you at the house by dinner."

"But—" she started to protest again.

"No negotiating. I need you and you will not let the family down. I need you to step up while Stanley recovers… if he ever recovers." Her father's voice broke and he coughed. "Come home, Tali. I need you," he finished softly.

Tali looked at the sketchbook sitting open on the bed where she'd left it earlier. It was open to the drawing she'd done while in the restaurant—the one with Gavin leaning against the railing looking over the city. She flipped the book closed and put a pillow over it so she wouldn't have to look at it while her heart crumbled and her dreams evaporated.

"Okay. I'll see you soon."

Tali hung up the phone and dialed Cameron before she had the chance to change her mind. He picked up after a few rings sounding very sleepy.

"Hey, Cam. My father called. There's a crisis and I need to head home right away. Can we get a flight scheduled for first thing in the morning?"

"Yeah, sure we can. But why did you call me instead of Captain Taylor? He's the one who's going to have to make the arrangements."

She couldn't stomach telling him herself, that's why.

Tali's heart constricted in her chest at the thought of telling Gavin she was going back.

She was far too much of a coward to stand up to her father for what she really wanted. She didn't want to hear the disappointment in Gavin's voice when he found out how weak she really was. There was no way Gavin would ever understand the choices she had to make for her family.

"Just make it happen, okay?"

"Okay. I'll let you know when we're leaving."

"Thanks." She hung up the phone and curled up on her side, pulling her covers over her head.

Tears rolled down her cheeks and soaked into the pillow beneath her head. Seemed she was going back to the States the same way she'd left—brokenhearted and alone.

Chapter Ten

Gavin stood on the top step of the stairs leading up to the cabin area of the small jet and looked across the tarmac at the terminal. Was she here yet?

He'd been woken in the middle of the night by Cameron saying they were to immediately fly back to the States at Tali's request. He was given no reason why. He could only assume she was done with him and was ready to return home to her real life—a life that didn't include him.

Well, he had no one to blame but himself. He deserved the pain growing in his chest for the awful things he'd said to Tali. He couldn't fault her for her choice, but he couldn't help but wish she'd made the choice to follow her heart. Instead, she was returning to a job she hated and a life that left her unsatisfied.

That she hadn't called him to schedule

them leaving, was more proof to him she was over him. She'd moved on and he was going to have to follow her lead. How he would move on without her, he wasn't sure.

The thought of not spending time with Tali made him feel unsatisfied, too. He'd miss her company, even if her company was a bit on the spoiled side and always full of smart-assed comments. He sighed.

He'd miss that ass of hers, too.

He straightened his back and forced himself to smile as a black town car drove up to plane. He would greet Tali like he did all his other passengers and he would keep his thoughts to himself. If she didn't want to be with him, he wasn't going to make a fool of himself trying to win her back. Well, at least he hoped he'd be strong enough not to make a fool of himself.

Tali stepped out of the back of the car and his stomach did a flip. She looked as beautiful as always. Her hair was piled on top of her head in a messy lump, and she wore a simple T-shirt and jeans. But somehow she looked amazing nonetheless.

Play it cool.

"Tali," he said simply as she walked passed him and into the plane.

She smiled over her shoulder as she made her way to her seat. "Captain Taylor."

Formalities. Not good.

"Can I help you with your bags or anything?" It was a professional enough question, wasn't it?

"No, thank you," she said, bending over to shove her bag into the space under her seat. Her ass looked great in those jeans. "Me and my—cargo—are already taken care of."

His gaze flickered up to her eyes from where it had settled happily on her rear. She grinned at him and the familiar twinkle of playfulness in her eyes lingered beneath the surface. Maybe she wasn't mad at him after all. Maybe there was still a chance for them to work things out.

She settled herself into her seat and Gavin moved to take the one next to her. "We have a few minutes before we're scheduled to leave and there's something I wanted to talk to you about."

She held up her hands. "Before you tell me what a mistake I'm making going back, you should know I don't have a choice this time."

"You always have choices, but that's not what I wanted to talk about. Tali, I—" Gavin's words were cut short as Tali gasped and looked past him to the door of the plane.

"What the hell are you doing here?" she asked.

Gavin turned to see a man walking toward them. Gavin stepped in the man's way and put his hands up. "Hold on a second. I don't have anyone else scheduled for this flight. Who are you and what are you doing on my plane?"

"That's Roger."

Roger? This was the dickhead who'd been stupid enough to cheat on Tali and then get engaged to his mistake. Gavin felt his blood pressure rising.

"I am on your passenger list. Check it again." Roger pushed passed him and took a seat across the small aisle from Tali. A grin spread across his face as he leaned back against the seat and folded his hands behind his head. "Hey, how about we get this show on the road, huh, Captain? Off you go. Flight checks and all that."

Gavin fisted his hands at his side. What the hell was going on? Why was Tali's ex on this flight all of a sudden? Why was he even in Paris to begin with when it sounded like Tali had left him back in the States?

"What are you doing on my flight?" He kept his voice calm and professional.

"Oh, didn't Tali tell you? She told me to head back to the States and when I heard she was headed back today too I figured we might as well share the ride. It's such a long trip to take in a private plane all on your own. It's much more fun to have someone special flying with you."

"Roger, I never—" Tali started.

Gavin cut her off mid-sentence. "Great. Glad to have you on board. I'll go do my final flight check and we'll be on our way in a few minutes."

"Gavin, wait," Tali called after him, but he disappeared out the door and down the stairs before he had to listen to her say anything else.

If she wanted to be with the jerk who had dumped her only a few days ago, then it was her business. Obviously she must have called him last night after their fight in the park. Well, thank God he hadn't gotten the chance to say what he'd planned.

Gavin finished checking the outside of the aircraft and returned to the interior of the plane. He tried not to pay attention to Tali and Roger, but he couldn't help but notice they were speaking. And it didn't sound like an argument.

Damn. Couldn't she have given him a heads up at least? Couldn't she have refrained from sleeping with Gavin if she thought there was a possibility she'd get back together with her ex?

Gavin closed the cockpit door so he wouldn't have to see them anymore. He reached into his pant pocket and pulled out the small square box he'd tucked away earlier. He'd planned on talking to Tali and giving it to her before they took off for the States. That wasn't going to happen now.

Expensive souvenir.

He stuffed the little box into his coat hanging in the small closet and closed the door tight. The little box would be safest tucked away where he didn't have to see it, feel it, or think about it. Now wasn't the time to dwell on such things. Not when he had a transatlantic flight to focus on.

As they taxied out onto the runway, Gavin couldn't help but feel as if maybe he wouldn't want to return to Paris again anytime soon. There were too many memories made in the last few days.

No. The city, the memories—Tali—all of it was better off left behind.

"Seriously, what the hell are you doing on my flight? How did you even find out I was on my way home today?" Tali scowled at Roger. Of all the ways Roger could decide to get his cheating self home to the States, he had to choose her way.

"I have my sources."

"Great. Good for you. You could have taken your own family's jet. You didn't have to hitchhike on mine."

"True, but it's such a long flight and we were going to the same place. I figured why not fly home together instead and then we're not alone."

"I like alone. Alone is a good thing. Why didn't you go on your own plane?"

"They'd already left to pick up my sister and her friends in Morocco. If I didn't go home with you, I'd have been stranded in Paris." He looked at her with his best doe-eyes, but she wasn't falling for it.

"Do you really think I'd care if you were stranded on a deserted island after what you did to me?"

He shook his head. "Tali, stop this. Stop acting like you're not happy to see me."

She laughed. He had some nerve. "I'm not happy to see you. This is not an act."

"We both know you're making me pay for what I did and that's okay," he continued as if he hadn't heard her. "I'll pay my dues a little longer until you feel satisfied and then we can move past this whole messy mix-up."

Seriously? Some nerve. "You cheated on me then got engaged. There's no mix-up there. And the thing that would satisfy me most right now is if you'd strap a parachute to your back and find out first-hand what it's like to fly."

"Oh, ouch. You always did have a mean streak. God I love that about you."

He crossed the aisle and took the seat next to her. She tried to shrink back against the outside wall of the plane. She didn't have any desire to be so close to him.

"I don't love anything about you anymore."

"Tali, come on now. There's no reason for you to act like this. Once we get home and back into the usual swing of things, you'll see you still have those feelings for me. You need to get over this already." He put his hand on her knee and squeezed. She cringed.

"You need to get the hell away from me. I'm not getting back into life as usual once I'm back home. I'm not going to be back home for long."

Roger's brow wrinkled. "What are you talking about?"

"Nothing, never mind." Shit. Why had she let that slip? She hadn't even figured out what she was going to do yet, she only knew she couldn't work for her father forever.

"Tell me what's going on."

"It's nothing. I just—" Damn it. Why had she opened her big mouth? "I thought about some stuff while I was away and I decided I don't want to work for my father's company anymore. I'm only going back now because Stanley had a heart attack and my dad needs the help for a little while."

"Really?" He smirked. "And what does daddy think about your decision?"

"He's not happy. He thinks I'm going to stay, but I'm not. I can't."

Roger slapped his hand across his thigh and laughed. "Well, this is fantastic news."

"I'm not so sure my father is going to agree with you, but great. Thanks for being surprisingly supportive."

"This is perfect. Now you can tell your dad how perfect I would be to take your place at the company. I could be his right-hand man and you could go do whatever weird thing it is you have your heart set on doing."

"Oh no. You know my father. 'The business started in this family and it'll stay in this family,'" she said in her most fatherly-sounding voice. "There's no way he'd ever let you step in for me."

The grin fell off of Roger's face as fast as it had appeared. "True. That does sound like something he'd say." He looked off into the distance and Tali started to relax.

Maybe now he'd leave her alone and go back to his own seat. Tali squeaked as he grabbed her hand and got down on one knee in front of her seat. So much for leaving her alone.

"Tali, marry me." He kissed the back of her hand and she thought she might throw up a little bit in her mouth.

"No," she managed to choke out. "No frickin' way."

"Yes. Don't you see? If you marry me, then I'll be a part of the family. Then your dad won't care if I take over your responsibility at the company, and you'll be free to go and do whatever it is you want to do. It's brilliant."

"It's the most ridiculous thing I've ever heard you say." She pulled her hand back from his and wrapped her arms around herself protectively. "Get up. I'm not going to marry you."

"Why not? It's a great idea." He took the seat beside her again and leaned into her, invading her personal space. "We'll make it work. We could consummate the relationship once or twice for the purpose of giving your parents grandbabies and then we'd both be free to live our own lives."

"Oh my God. I can't believe you're actually saying these things. Do you hear yourself? No way. To any of it. I don't want you taking my job. I don't want to marry you and I certainly don't want to make babies with you. Gah, the thought is enough to make me celibate."

"That's uncalled for." Roger softened his expression and twirled a piece of her hair in his fingers. "Think about it. Your dad would be happy. I would be happy. You could do your silly art or whatever. You owe it to your father to find a way to give him a capable successor and we both know that person has always been me."

Tali's pulse pounded in her ears as the

anger she felt for Roger consumed her. How dare he imply she wasn't a capable successor? Capabilities and skill had nothing to do with her choice to not work for her father. She was more than ready and able to do the job asked of her—she simply didn't want to.

"You're an asshole and you need to get the hell away from me before I clip you in your man jewels again."

"Now, now. Let's not say things we're going to regret. You know if I'd asked you this question a week ago, you would've said yes. You would be pulling off your clothes to jump into bed with me. So let's not go on pretending those feelings aren't there when we both know they are. Just say yes so we can move on to the make-up sex part."

"No. Absolutely—" Tali's protest was cut off as Roger crushed his mouth to hers. *Really? Not again.* "Get off," she demanded against his mouth, but her words were garbled as he stuck his tongue into her mouth, forcefully exploring her.

His fingers, which only moments before had been gently twirling strands of her hair, were now tangled in her thick mane. The fine hairs at the base of her skull screamed in pain as his grip tightened, pulling the hairs taut. His other hand cupped her breast, squeezing and kneading the tender flesh in ways that should have been appealing. But given the current situation, all she felt was fear rising in her throat.

This was worse than in the hotel room. Roger had her pinned between the wall and the seats and she had nowhere to go—no leverage to wiggle out from beneath him. Damn it, no way to get her knee to connect with the one place she knew would make him stop.

Roger dropped his hand from the back of her head and roughly pulled down the shoulder of her shirt, exposing the top of her breast to the cold cabin air. He kissed a path along her jaw, hungrily nibbling her collarbone as he made his way to her breast.

She opened her mouth to scream, but no words came out. Tears pooled in her eyes, blurring her vision. Her thoughts spun out of control. How could this be happening with Gavin so close?

Gavin.

She blinked away her tears and focused on the cockpit door. Please hear me.

"Help," she yelled as loud as she could, but her voice came out strained, barely more than a whispered.

"Oh, yeah, babe. I'll help you. You help me right now, then I'll help you get daddy to understand."

No. She wasn't going to let this happen. She strained her body beneath him, trying to wiggle free or throw him off of her in any way she could.

"Gavin," she yelled. This time her voice was loud and clear. A moment later she heard the cockpit door open and slam into the wall.

Chapter Eleven

"What the fuck?" Gavin cursed at the sight of Roger on top of Tali, her hands pounding his chest and back. Her eyes met his for a fraction of a second and he instantly knew why she'd called out to him. She needed help.

He gripped Roger by the shoulders and pulled him off of Tali, freeing her. She scrambled back toward the window, looking tiny in the oversized seat. He attempted to keep the fury out of his voice as he spoke. "What the hell is going on here?"

"None of your business, dip shit. That's what," Roger said, puffing up his chest. The gesture did little good as Gavin towered over him.

I could break him like a twig.

"Return to your seat," Gavin said through clenched teeth. *Keep it together.*

"Sure, no problem." Roger moved to sit

in the free seat beside Tali and she shrank away from him, pressing her back against the outer wall of the plane.

"Not that seat." Gavin pointed across the aisle to the seat Roger had originally sat in at the beginning of the flight. "That seat." No way was he going to let Roger sit anywhere near Tali when she was so obviously scared of him. And he couldn't blame her.

Roger smiled and turned on the charm. Gavin was sure Roger used his moderate good looks and his stuffed wallet on anyone he wanted anything from. Little shit probably usually succeeded too. But not this time.

"Come on, man." Roger patted Gavin on the shoulder as if they were lifelong buddies. "We're all friends here. Tali doesn't mind the company do you, babe? What with our new engagement and all, we've been using the flight to get reacquainted with each other."

"Engagement?" Gavin directed his

question at Tali. No way. That wasn't possible.

She shook her head. "No. He asked and I said no, then he forced himself on me." Her voice cracked as she said the words.

The vein in Gavin's neck pulsed as his heartbeat raced. He could practically see the fury clouding his judgment, but he forced it away. As long as he was pilot of this aircraft, he had to remain in control, no matter what situation came up.

He turned to Roger, grabbed him by the arm and not so gently tossed him toward his seat. *That's control, right? I didn't punch him.*

"You will sit your butt in your seat for the remainder of the flight and keep your thoughts—and hands—to yourself or you'll find a sky marshal waiting for you on the tarmac when we arrive in the States. Understand?"

Roger nodded and fastened his seatbelt before turning to face the window. Gavin took a few deep breaths, forcing himself to stay calm.

He could beat the crap out of Roger after they were safely on the ground in the States. For now he'd have to be content to threaten him—threats he would happily follow through with later.

Gavin sat in the seat next to Tali and wrapped her in his arms. "Are you okay?" he asked her softly.

She nodded and gripped his shirt in her hands. "I'm fine now. Thanks to you."

"I'll always protect you." He kissed her on the forehead. "What happened? Did he really ask you to marry him?"

She pulled away from him a little and he could see the pain behind her eyes. She opened her mouth to speak, but before she could, Cameron the co-pilot spoke over the intercom.

"Captain Taylor, you're needed up front immediately, please."

The line crackled for a minute as Gavin waited to hear more, but nothing further was said. Odd. Normally Cameron would tell him what he needed.

"I better head up front and check this out. Cameron's a great co-pilot, but he can only be in charge of the controls for so long. We'll continue this conversation when we land, okay?"

"Okay. Do you think something's wrong?"

"I'm sure everything is fine, not to worry." He stroked his hand along her jaw and gave her a quick, soft kiss on the cheek. The tingle of her skin against his mouth was enough to stir the familiar fiery heat in his groin, but that too would have to wait.

He stood and strode back to the cockpit door, then turned back to his passengers. Leveling Roger with a stare that hopefully evoked a bit of fear, Gavin addressed his next comment at him alone. "If you try anything—even speaking to Tali while this plane is still in the air, I swear I'll have an air marshal waiting when the door opens. Don't push me. Got it?"

Roger grunted a reply and sunk down into his seat a little further.

"Good."

* * * *

Tali sat with her eyes closed, gripping the armrests of her seat with both hands. Her white knuckles ached under the pressure. She gasped when the plane jumped with turbulence as they approached the runway.

The last half of the flight had been troublesome. Not only because Roger was a complete asshole and forced himself on her, but also because they'd run into a large weather system stretching almost the entire length of the US coastline and covering a large portion of the Atlantic. Gavin had warned them shortly after returning to the cabin of the approaching weather and had assured her they would be fine.

As much as she believed and trusted him, it was impossible not to be nervous as the plane bounced around above the Atlantic Ocean like a pinball in the clouds. She did her best to stay calm and wondered how on Earth Gavin managed to stay cool in the face of so much pressure. He was so much stronger than she could ever hope to be.

Tali felt the telltale bump of the aircrafts wheels hitting the runway and sighed deeply with relief. Outside, rain streamed down the windows and covered the ground beside the runway in puddles. Off in the distance she could see blue sky beginning to break through. The storm had almost passed.

"So that's it then?" Roger asked, breaking into her thoughts. He'd been silent the rest of the flight. She'd almost forgotten he was still on the plane. "You're going to walk away from your family and everything they've been working for and run off with this pilot. This blue-collar nobody."

"Yep. You've got me all figured out." She held her breath and counted. She didn't want to talk to Roger about her decision anymore. The choice was hers to make, and she'd made it. Any doubt she'd had back in Paris was gone.

Now she knew what people like Roger were willing to do to someone else to get what they wanted. No. She could never be happy if she were a part of that world. Her dad would have to figure something else out.

Roger grunted.

Sexy.

"You're disgusting," he sneered. "I always knew you were selfish but this is too much, even for you."

The jet came to a stop and the engines shut down.

"I think it's time for you to get on with your own life and leave me alone." Tali glared at Roger, daring him to try something again. Now they were back on the ground and she could have help here in seconds to haul him away. *Go ahead. Just try it.*

"Afraid I can't do that. See I already emailed your father and requested a meeting. Soon, your father and I will be like this," he said, twining his fingers together. "He'll be so thankful to finally have the son he always wanted."

Tali narrowed her eyes at him. No way. There was no way she was going to let Roger treat her this way, then waltz into her family like he had a right to be there. Nope.

"You're going to email my father and cancel your meeting or I'm going to tell my father and the cops what you did to me on this plane. What you would have accomplished if Gavin hadn't come to my rescue. So unless you want your name splattered across the news and magazines about how you're an attempted rapist,

I'd suggest you move on quickly and quietly."

"I hate you."

"Not as much as I loathe you."

The cockpit door opened and Gavin strode out looking even more amazing than Tali remembered. Maybe it was the bumpy flight or maybe it was the realization about what she really wanted in life, but Tali couldn't wait to be with him again—forever, if he'd have her.

"Do I need to radio for the air marshal or are you ready to leave quietly?"

Roger rose from his seat. "I'm going. Have a nice life, Tali. I hope you're happy ten years from now when your trust fund runs out and your 'art' has to sustain you. Mr Blue-collar himself certainly won't be able to."

With that, Roger stepped through the open door and descended the steps without waiting for her to reply, which was fine with her since she didn't have anything left to say to him anyway. The only one she needed to talk to now stood right in front of her.

She swallowed hard, suddenly nervous at the prospect of what could happen with their conversation. Good or bad—whether he thought she was making the right choice or not, she wanted to tell him what she'd decided to do. Her decision was final.

"Did you still want to talk?" She mumbled the words as her nervousness got the better of her. "I think you said that before the turbulence. Or, um, if you don't want to talk, that's fine too. I can go. I should probably go, right?"

She reached for her handbag and shouldered it as she made her way quickly toward the open door. She was stupid to think he'd still want to talk to her after everything she'd said to him. It would be better for everyone if she left now before more was said that couldn't be taken back.

"Wait," Gavin said, putting his arm up

across the entrance, blocking her path to the door. "I do still want to talk. Will you stay?"

Hope sprang into her chest, her head going slightly dizzy with possibility. Of course she would stay if he wanted to talk. How could she refuse him when she wanted to work things out?

How could she refuse when he stood so close to her, towering over her in the small jet—the scent of his now-familiar cologne filling the tiny space? She could smell his scent for a million years and never tire of it. If that were actually to happen, she'd have to build up some kind of tolerance to it since her knees were suddenly threatening to go weak on her again.

Every. Time.

"Yeah, sure. I can stay for a few minutes." That was casual enough, right?

"Good."

She expected a smile from him, but his solemn face didn't crack. This probably wasn't going to be the conversation she'd hoped to have. She could feel her happiness, her hope, sliding away like the smile on her own face. Tears from concern, from stress, or from all of the crappy emotional shit she'd been through over the last few days, pricked the backs of her eyes, threatening to spill down her cheeks. Again.

She swallowed the hopelessness rising in her throat. No. She wasn't going to break down and cry. She deserved whatever it was she would get from Gavin. Now wasn't the time to cry. Now was the time to put on her big girl panties and take whatever heartbreak she was given.

"It's that Kerry girl, isn't it? I slapped you and then you ran off into her arms. I understand and I deserve it. Just tell me so I can move on."

Gavin leaned in, narrowing the gap between them, his eyes never leaving hers. "I don't want anything to do with Kerry."

Woo hoo!

His face was so close to hers now she could feel his breath on her lips. Maybe this conversation wouldn't be a conversation after all. Maybe they'd skip the boring talking and move directly to the make-up sex part instead. That part was always more fun than talking ever would be.

She licked her lips, trying to capture the faintest hint of his breath on her tongue. To taste him the way she'd been longing to since they'd first been together. His lips parted as if to answer her unspoken need for him.

"We done here, boss?" Cameron asked, stepping out of the cockpit and completely killing the moment.

She groaned, unable to stop herself before the sound was out of her body and floating in the air around them.

Cameron's gaze flickered back and forth

between Gavin and Tali, taking in their close proximity. "Sorry to interrupt. I'll get out of here." Finally, he understood and would leave so Tali wouldn't have to kick him out of the plane.

He disappeared before either of them had a chance to confirm or deny his assumption. It didn't matter what he thought anyway. The only one who mattered right now was Gavin. The air was silent and thick between them as Cameron's footsteps faded away. The quiet was too much for her.

"I'm sorry," she said quickly before Gavin had the chance to speak. "I'm sorry for being such a spoiled brat. I'm sorry for treating you like a servant, for yelling at you when you were only trying to help me. For everything, I'm so sorry."

Her breath hitched in her throat as she fought her tears, waiting agonizingly long seconds for him to respond. But instead of replying like she expected him to, he pressed his lips to hers. Her head swam with confusion and happiness mixed into one giant ball of crazy. She didn't know why he was kissing her, but she didn't care.

Tali ran her hands up his chest and gripped his tailored shirt in her fists, pulling him closer to her—as close as she could possibly get him. She wanted to taste him, touch him, savor every inch of him.

His tongue plunged into her mouth, exploring her. She groaned in response, arching into him and wrapping her hands around his head, tugging on his short hair. A growl of pleasure came from him, sending a spike of heat through her body. God, she loved this man.

I love him?

Tali giggled into his mouth. The instant pleasure of realizing how she really felt was amazing. She couldn't believe it took her so long to figure it out for herself, but it had. She loved

Gavin and the thought of losing him and how it tore her up inside, was merely proof of that. She giggled again, happiness making her feel as if she were drunk.

Gavin pulled away from her and peered into her eyes, his brow creased with confusion. "What's so funny?" His voice was husky with need. "This isn't exactly a good time to laugh."

Tali laughed out loud. Damn he was cute. *And I love him!*

"I'm sorry. It's not funny but I can't help laughing. I just realized the most ridiculous thing—I love you." She gasped, covering her mouth with her hand. Had she really just put that out there for him to hear? She could almost see the words lingering in the air.

"You love me?" he asked.

She nodded. Yep. God help her, she loved him in a way she'd never experienced before.

She bit her lip as he studied her. What if

he didn't love her back? What if he'd only been kissing her goodbye forever and wanted nothing else to do with her?

"I know I haven't treated you very well," she said, "and I haven't been very honest with myself about who I am and what I want in life. I don't expect you to love me back, not when I'm only just learning to love myself. I'll understand if you want to ignore what I said and walk away from me. I'll—"

"Shut up, woman, and kiss me." He pulled her against him, cupping her butt with one hand so her body pressed fully against his. "I love you, too," he whispered.

He pressed his mouth to hers gently at first as if trying to tease her. His tongue flicked across her lips. His free hand disappeared under her shirt, quickly unfastening her bra with ease. Skimming his hand over her flesh, he left a path of tingles in his wake. He kneaded her breast and thumbed her nipple.

"I love you too, Tali," he again said, pulling back from her enough to get the words out. His forehead rested against hers as his hands continued to explore her body. "Since the first moment in the cockpit when I learned your mouth was just as hot tempered as my own, I knew you were the one for me. I just kept trying to fight it. I'm stupid."

"No, you were right to fight your feelings. I wasn't ready." She ran her hand along his jaw, cupping it. "You were right about me. I wasn't being honest with myself or my family about what I really wanted in life. I tried to live a lie that would never make me truly happy. You—you showed me I can be who I really am and it's okay. That's why I'm going to tell my father he needs to find someone to replace me. I won't be taking over the job of running the company."

"Really? Are you sure? I thought we were coming home because your father needed you, some crisis or something."

"There is a crisis. He does need me and I won't let him down right now. But I will tell him I'll only help until Stanley is on his feet again or until I hire someone to fill my spot. Then I'm to be set free. For the first time ever in my life, I'll be free to do what I choose to do and not what's been chosen for me. And I owe it all to you, Gavin."

"I'm so proud of you. And I'll be with you every step of the way—if you'll let me."

"I wouldn't have it any other way. Besides," she giggled. "Who else would I have fly me all over the world to paint my great masterpieces?"

"Sounds like you're going to need a frequent flyer card."

"True. Maybe I'll even become a member of the mile-high club."

"That might be tricky when I'm the guy flying the plane." He laughed.

She grinned. "Isn't that what auto-pilot is for?"

"Good thinking. How about we practice once before we try it at thirty thousand feet?"

He pulled her down into one of the large leather seats, her legs straddling his thighs. She slipped her shirt and bra over her head and let them fall onto the floor in a heap. The cold air from the open door caressed her skin, raising little goose bumps.

"Shouldn't we close the door?"

He shrugged. "Probably, but that would mean moving and I'm not too interested in doing that right now. Beside, we're in the private hanger area; no one ever bothers me when I'm finishing up after a flight. No one will bother us now."

"You like the thrill of possibly getting caught, don't you?" she teased.

"It doesn't *not* thrill me."

She hit him playfully and folded her

arms across her bare breasts as she stood. "Go close the door and I'll wait right here. I'm not into getting caught. I have a reputation as being a stone cold bitch to hold on to, remember?"

"Got it."

Gavin quickly closed the cabin door and then briefly disappeared into the cockpit before returning to his seat. She climbed into his lap again. "Where did you go?"

"To get this." Gavin placed a small square box in her hand. "I have a little something for you I picked up in Paris before we left. Open it."

Suspicion flared to life in Tali's brain. What was he doing? It was too early for giving a gift that came in a tiny square box. A little velvet box to be exact.

"Gavin, I can't. I—I'm not ready. Hell, I only figured out I love you a few minutes ago. I can't accept this." She tried to shove the box back into his hand.

"It's not what you think and you can accept it. I promise, I'm not proposing while you're topless, although there is a certain appeal to that scenario."

Tali held her breath as she opened the little box. Inside was the pendent she'd seen displayed in the window of one of the boutiques along the Champs-Élysées the day she'd made Gavin go shopping with her. It was the most amazing pendant she'd ever seen. How had he known how much she'd loved it?

"The moment I saw you looking at it with that twinkle in your eyes, was the moment I suspected there was more to you than you let on. I knew in that instant I had to find out who you really were and I'm so glad I did.

"You, Tali, are as unique as this pendant. You said it was a perfect piece because each person who gazed on it would see something different. I saw a bunch of swirls, but you saw possibility. Never stop seeing possibility in everything."

Tali nodded. Her throat constricted with tears and love and an unbelievable respect for this man who knew her better than she even knew herself. She leaned forward so Gavin could fasten the necklace around her neck. As the cold metal pendant hit her chest directly above her heart, it instantly warmed to her skin. She glanced down at the colorful design then back into Gavin's eyes. In them, she saw all the possibility she'd ever need in life. In them she saw her future.

The End

ALSO BY HEATHER THURMEIER

Available at **Silver Publishing**:

MEADOW RIDGE ROMANCES
Love and Lattes
Love on Landing

CPSIA information can be obtained at www.ICGtesting.com
Printed in the USA
LVOW081907270512

283465LV00001B/65/P

9 781614 954750